Still grieving over the sudden death of his lover, antiques dealer Flynn Ambrose moves to the old, ramshackle house on Pitch Pine Lane to catalog and sell the large inventory of arcane and oddball items that once filled his late uncle's mysterious museum.

But not all the items are that easy to catalog. Or get rid of...

The Haunted Heart series. Four seasons. Four ghosts. Two hearts.

Winter. Since Alan died, Flynn isn't eating, isn't sleeping, and isn't spending a lot of time looking in mirrors. But maybe he should pay a little more attention — because something in that 18th Century mirror is looking at *him*.

THE
HAUNTED
HEART:
WINTER

JOSH LANYON

THE HAUNTED HEART: WINTER

August 2013

ISBN-10: 1-937909-55-7

ISBN-13: 978-1-937909-55-0

Published in the United States of America

Just Joshin

3053 Rancho Vista Blvd.

Suite 116

Palmdale, CA 93551

www.joshlanyon.com

This is a work of fiction. Any resemblance to persons living or dead is entirely coincidental.

TABLE OF CONTENTS

Let us be grateful to the mirror for revealing to us our appearance only.

— **Samuel Butler**

CHAPTER ONE

I didn't see him until it was too late.

A tall, faceless figure looming up out of the shadows. Even if I had seen him, I'm not sure it would have made a difference. My only thought was getting downstairs and out the front door as fast as possible. It turned out the fastest way was crashing headlong into someone bigger, and letting my momentum send us both hurtling down the staircase.

My...er...companion yelled and cursed all the way down the first flight. Well, in fairness it was one long yelp and a prolonged curse. *"Yooouuu've gotta be fu-uh-uh-uh-uh-cking kid-ding me!"*

We landed in a tangle of limbs on the unswept and none-too-plushy carpet. My elbow whanged one final time into the balusters and my head banged down on the floor. I saw stars. Or maybe that was just the dust, which had probably crystallized with age.

"What the hell was *that*?" moaned someone from the ether.

Good. Question.

What the hell *had* that been? It sure wasn't a trick of the light. Though I'd done my best to tell myself that's exactly what it was — and had kept telling myself that right up until the moment the murkiness in the mirror had begun to take form.

"Sorry about that," I mumbled. His bare foot was planted in my gut, and I couldn't blame him when he dug his toes in for leverage before lifting off me. *"Oof!"*

"What do you think you're doing running down these stairs in the middle of the night?"

I groped for the railing and pulled myself painfully into a sitting position. "I... thought someone was in my room." Lying was second nature to me by now, but that was a stupid lie. I knew it, the instant the words left my mouth.

404-A — What was his name? Something Murdoch — got to his knees and gaped at me in the dingy light. "Why didn't you say so?"

"I am saying so."

We both turned to stare up at the wide-open door leading into my rooms. My lamp-lit and noticeably silent rooms.

We looked at each other.

404-A was older than me, bigger than me, shaggier than me. He had a beard and shoulder length black hair. His eyes were dark and sort of hollow looking — that was probably lack of sleep. He looked like those old posters for *Serpico,* but he wasn't a cop. He was some kind of a writer.

And a crap guitarist. Then again, I wasn't anyone's dream neighbor either. As indicated by current events.

"You think someone's up there?" He asked me slowly, skeptically.

I weighed a possible visit from the local fuzz, and opted for resident whacko.

"I did. But...maybe I was wrong."

"Maybe? *Maybe?* Why don't we find out?" He was on his feet now, yanking his red plaid flannel bathrobe shut and retying it with a couple of hard, businesslike tugs that vaguely suggested a wish to throttle something. Without waiting to see if I was following or not, he stomped up the flight of stairs. Guiltily, I noticed he was limping.

It was actually amazing either of us hadn't been seriously injured or even killed in that fall.

"Coming?" he threw over his shoulder.

"Uh..."

He muttered something, and not pausing for an answer, disappeared through the doorway.

I admit I waited.

He couldn't fail to see the mirror first thing. It was as tall as I was, cartouche-shaped, mounted on an ornate, ormolu frame. It stood propped against a Chinese black lacquer curio cabinet. The slight angle created the effect of walking up a slanted floor to peer into its silvered surface.

An icy draft whispered against the back of my neck. I shivered. This dilapidated four-story Victorian monstrosity was full of drafts. Drafts and dust. And shadows and creaks. All of them perfectly harmless. I shivered again.

Footsteps squeaked overhead. "It's clear. Come on up. There's nobody here," 404-A called at last.

I let out a long breath and jogged up the stairs. The elfin faces carved in the black walnut railing winked and smirked at me as I passed.

I reached the top landing and walked into the jumble sale of my living room. "Living room" was kind of a euphemism. It was more like the entry hall of a failing museum, complete with battered statuary and oil paintings of morose Flemish people. And in fact most of these objects had been in a museum at one time. My late great Great-Uncle Winston's museum of weirdness.

My gaze fell on the mirror first thing, but the surface showed only me, tall and skinny and pale in my Woody Woodpecker boxers. My hair looked like Woody's too, only blond, not red. Definitely standing on end, whatever the color.

"I guess I dreamed…it," I said by way of apology.

"First time living alone?" 404-A asked dryly. He stood right beside the mirror, his own reflection off to the side.

"Ha," I said. "Not hardly." But come to think of it, he was right. I'd lived at home until college and then after college, I'd lived with Alan. This was my first time totally on my own. "Anyway, sorry about dragging you out of bed and knocking you down the stairs. Are you sure you're okay?"

"*I'm* fine." He continued to eye me in a way that seemed a bit clinical.

Yeah. I got the message. Maybe I *had* dreamed it. What a relief to realize it was just a nightmare.

If only I slept.

"Come to think of it, you were already on your way up here," I remembered.

He said bluntly, "I was going to ask you to stop pacing up and down all night. The floorboards creak."

"*Oh.*" My face warmed at this rude but effective reminder that I wasn't alone in the world. Not even this crumbly and dimly lit corner of the world. "Sorry," I mumbled. To be honest, I forgot he was even in the building most of the time. He was pretty quiet, other than the occasional fit of guitar picking, and it was just the two of us here at 404 Pitch Pine Lane. We were neither of us the sociable type.

I glanced at the mirror again. Just me and the edge of my neighbor's plaid bathrobe in its shining surface. The reflection of the ceiling chandelier blazed like a sunspot in the center, obliterating most of us and the room we stood in.

I looked more closely. Had something moved in the very back of the reverse room?

404-A glanced down at the mirror and then back at me. He said, "I have to work tomorrow."

"Sure. I didn't realize you could hear me."

He unbent enough to say, "I mostly can't. Only the floorboards. Mainly at night."

"I'll make sure to pace in the other room."

"Great." He pushed away from the cabinet and headed for the door. "I'll let you get back to it."

His reflection crossed the mirror's surface, large bare feet, ragged Levi's beneath the hem of the bathrobe.

"Night," I said absently. I remembered to ask, "What's your name again?"

"Murdoch. Kirk Murdoch."

Kirk Murdoch? Try saying that five times fast. Not that I planned on making a habit of calling for Kirk. "Right. Night, Kirk."

"Goodnight, Flynn."

I watched the mirrored reflection of the door closing quietly behind him.

CHAPTER TWO

Sleep. That's what I needed. A good night's sleep.

I continued to stand there watching the mirror.

Nothing moved. Not in my room. Not in the mirrored room.

I waited.

Waited.

It could have been clouds drifting past the window. Or the way the drafts pushed the shadows around the room.

Maybe I *had* dreamed it.

Or, more likely, the lack of sleep was catching up with me.

But what if — just maybe — I'd got it all wrong? What if what I'd seen, thought I'd seen, had been the answer to a prayer?

I watched the mirror for another minute. The cold silence of the house began to get to me. It was late. Past midnight. I was tired. And probably starting to see things.

A tune came into my mind. *All we are say-ing...is give sleep a chance...*

I stepped back and turned off the overhead light. Darkness fell like a drop cloth, cloaking the crowded furniture and objets d'art. Here and there, starlight from the narrow sash windows glanced off a finial or cornice. Still watching the opaque surface of the mirror, I sat down on a brocade upholstered Napoleon III chair and leaned forward, staring closely.

"Are you there?" I whispered.

I couldn't be sure, but it seemed as though...perhaps...something changed, as though the darkness in the mirror wavered.

I rose from the chair, crossed the floor, knelt before the mirror. I peered at the silvered surface, eyes straining. Yes, there was motion, a roiling like dark smoke...

something stirring at the bottom of the mirror, moving in the opaque depths, walking up the tilted floor of the reverse room, coming toward me.

My breath caught. "Alan?"

For an instant everything was still. Very still. Then the darkness seemed to dissipate, disperse in the path of a pale illumination. My throat closed. My eyes stung. I leaned close, trying to peer through the glass.

There it was. A tiny glimmer, a pinprick of light, barely more than a spark. I could just make it out through the blur of my tears.

I wasn't imagining it. It was real. Tears welled. I wiped them away. I released a hard, shuddering breath.

"Alan..."

I put my hand to the mirror's surface, felt the glass warm beneath my skin. I pressed harder. The glass did not give. I closed my eyes, tried to picture it melting away beneath my hand, concentrated hard for long minutes, but it stayed firm and... cool.

Cool.

The glass was growing cold. I opened my eyes. The mirror was dark now, the surface so chill it stung like I was touching ice. A sob tore out of my throat. "Don't go!"

The mirror was black and empty, revealing nothing now but the bulky outlines of the furniture and my bowed figure. Impatiently, I mopped my eyes and nose.

But it wasn't a dream. I wasn't asleep. It had been real. I rested my head against the mirror, my breath misting the glass. *Come back. Come back...*

There was no sound. I don't know why I opened my eyes, but I did, and I saw — or at least had the impression — of someone walking up the tilted floor behind me.

I whirled, but there was no one there. Only starlight stippling empty floorboards, the gleam of the clock pendulum swinging hypnotically back and forth, the painted kiss on the lips of a porcelain nymph.

Heart pounding, I turned back to the mirror, but the image staring back at me was not my own.

Not me.

Something else was there, something gazed back, staring at me as though the mirror were a window. I leaned in, trying to see more clearly, and the translucent form slowly, slowly seemed to take solid shape.

A woman regarded me. She was maybe my age, mid-twenties, unexpectedly beautiful with a cloud of black hair and heavy-lidded eyes shining like jewels. She wore something pale and filmy. Or maybe that pale, filminess was her. I couldn't quite make it out.

"What are you?" I was thinking aloud, really, not expecting an answer.

And yet…there *was* something there. I didn't believe in an afterlife. But maybe I had been thinking of the afterlife the wrong way. Maybe this was a psychic echo, an imprint of energy, not alive, not intelligent or interactive…just an impression. Kind of like the indentation a pen makes on the paper below the page being written on.

This was just a tracing, a shadow of whatever she had once been.

No need to be frightened of a shadow. This was like studying a painting; she was as pretty as the Dresden nymph pirouetting on the mantelpiece.

But as I crouched there, watching her image waver in and out like a fading light bulb, an ominous feeling began to creep over me. A growing sense of dread. There was no reason for it, no tangible threat, but the sense of menace, of danger, mounted. My heart pounded in my throat, my hands felt cold and clammy, my stomach knotted in anxiety.

"What do you want?" I whispered shakily.

I didn't believe I was actually communicating with…it, so her smile — the patent amusement in that little mocking curl of her lip — knocked me literally back on my heels.

I scrambled up and she was laughing at me. Silently.

It shocked me. More. It terrified me.

This was what I had felt earlier, this feeling of something very wrong, something closing in on me. This was what had sent me rushing out of the room and down the stairs. My heart thundered in my chest as she floated there, seeming as real and immediate as myself, laughing at me as though she found my bewilderment amusing. No, it wasn't just the amusement. It was the derision behind it. Whatever she — it — was, it wasn't friendly.

I drew back — and then crawled still farther away — as she slowly, almost cautiously reached out.

I didn't wait to see if she breached the mirror's surface. I was on my feet, out the door, and flying down the stairs once more.

There was no bar of light under 404-A's door. I hammered on the scratched, battered surface anyway.

The door flew open before I reached the crescendo of my drum solo. Kirk Murdoch was hastily zipping up his jeans, his expression a blend of outrage and grievance. His hair looked like a bush and he had the kind of six-pack abs rarely seen on dudes who didn't make a living doing infomercials. One rock hard bicep bore the narrow red and black banner of a tattoo which read 75 RANGER RGT.

"There's something wrong upstairs," I told him.

"You're telling me!"

"I have to show you something. Will you come? Please?"

"*Now*?"

"Yes. Now. Sorry, but it has to be now."

Murdoch stared at me with hard, narrowed eyes.

"Please. Now," I urged when he showed no sign of moving.

"What are you on?" he asked at last, conversationally. "Didn't anybody teach you not to mix —"

"Nothing. I'm not drunk. I'm not on anything. I'm not —"

"When was the last time you slept?"

"If you'll just come with me, you'll see. If it's not there then...I don't know. Maybe I am crazy. But I'm not crazy. It *was* there."

"You seem crazy to me. No offense."

"We're wasting time," I pleaded.

"Why not? We have all night, judging by appearances."

I got control of myself. Took a deep breath. "Look, Murdoch — Kirk — I know how this looks."

"Probably not."

I said simply, desperately, "I need help."

After a nerve-wracking second or two, he reached back into the room and picked up a baseball bat. "Okay. Lead on, MacDuff. Let's get this over with."

This time I led the way up the stairs, though Murdoch was right on my heels. I was glad he hadn't brought the baseball bat the first time; it wouldn't have seemed a neighborly gesture. I hated to tell him I didn't think a bat would be any use now.

He held it with an easy and reassuring confidence that suggested he was practiced at hitting homeruns or splitting open heads as required. Not exactly my idea of the bookish type, but I didn't know any writers. In another life I had been an antique dealer.

Not *literally* another life. That seemed an important distinction at the moment.

We reached the top floor and the door to my rooms. I turned to Murdoch and whispered, "Look at the mirror." I pushed the door wide.

He made a strangled sound, but followed me without comment into the unlit room.

The mirror was dark.

Not an unnatural, mystical dark, just...dark. The triangle of feeble, grimy light from the hall sliced across its surface as I closed the door behind us.

Murdoch stood unmoving beside me, a bulky shape in the gloom. He smelled of liniment or something eucalyptus, and I was reminded of his — our — recent tumble down stairs. He was a nice guy, Murdoch. Even if he did look like a biker dude. To have followed me up here after our earlier encounter? That was kind.

He was quiet for such a big man. I couldn't even hear him breathing.

The clocks — seven of them at my last count — ticked loudly in the silence.

I kept my gaze trained on the mirror.

Nothing.

Not a gleam. Not a spark.

"What are we waiting for?" Murdoch asked at last, and the loudness of his normal speaking voice made me jump.

"Wait. Please. Just wait," I whispered.

"Wait for what?"

"*Shhh!*"

I felt him reach behind me. The chandelier blazed on overhead, leaving me blinking in its dazzle. "What the hell is going on?" Murdoch demanded. "What are we waiting for? What do you think is going to happen?"

"I can't explain it. You wouldn't believe me. It's better for you to see it yourself." I reached over and flipped off the light switch.

He flipped it back on. "No. It doesn't work like that, Mr. Ambrose. Explain to me what you think is going on. Or I'm going back to bed. Now."

I had been "Flynn" earlier. Now I was "Mr. Ambrose." I said, "You have to be patient."

"No. I don't. Tell me what's going on or I'm out of here."

Had something moved in the mirror? I stared more closely.

"Suit yourself." He turned to go.

"Wait." My hand clamped down on his arm, startling us both, I think.

"I saw something when I looked in the mirror," I told Murdoch.

He glanced at my hand, still gripping his forearm. I could feel hard ropes of tendon beneath the warmth of his skin. The last time I'd touched another man's bare skin, the man had been Alan. We had made love that morning. The last morning.

I didn't dare think about that now.

Murdoch was frowning at me. He shifted the frown to the mirror which framed us in the tilted room surrounded by the cabinets and candelabras and crystal.

"That's a good thing, isn't it?" he asked. "Wouldn't it be a bigger problem if you *didn't* have a reflection?"

I shook my head. "You think I'm crazy. This is why you have to see it for yourself."

"I don't know if you're crazy. I do know you haven't slept since you got here a week ago. And I know firsthand what the lack of sleep can do to someone."

There was probably an interesting story to go with that assertion. "I nap during the day," I answered, gazing once more at the mirror. It wasn't a lie. I did snatch cat naps now and then. Not for long. If I slept too long, I forgot that Alan was dead. And then when I woke up, I had to go through remembering all over again. That was the real reason I refused to take the meds. In the long run they made it harder.

I leaned my head to the right, then to the left. Side to side to see if I could somehow see past the room's reflection to what I knew waited behind.

I was startled when Murdoch twisted his arm so that now it was his big hand that was gripping me. "Fine," he said. "You want to do this, let's do it. You sit down here." He gave me a little push toward the Napoleon III chair.

I sat down, gazing doubtfully up at him.

He turned, flipped the switch on the chandelier, dousing the room in instant Cimmerian night. His disembodied voice floated over to me. "I'll sit over here." His bulky shadow crossed in front of the mirror and lowered to the long Queen Anne sofa. The sofa cushions huffed a musty protest I heard from across the room. "We've got our positions and we'll watch all night. How's that?"

"Are you — do you mean that?"

"Doesn't it look like I mean it?"

I watched his large silhouette lay the baseball bat on an end table, pick up the unicorn tapestry draped over the sideboard and spread it over himself like a blanket. Actually, it looked like he was settling down for the night.

"Are you going to sleep?" I asked.

"Nope. But if you have any sense, you will."

I started to answer, then cut myself off. Okay. Let him sleep. Maybe that was better. Maybe the mirror would cooperate now. And if something did happen, I could always sneak over there and shake him awake.

"Can you even see the mirror from there?"

"I can see it all quite clearly," he said grimly, and I was surprised to hear myself laugh.

CHAPTER THREE

A strange, low voice growled, "The hell?"

My eyes flew open. I'd been resting them. Just for a minute or two. At least, I'd only thought it was a minute or two, but in the gloom I could make out a bulky form crouched a few feet from me.

Memory snapped back into place and I sat up. The bulky form was Murdoch. He was kneeling in front of the mirror. The mirror was still dark. Too dark. The room was no longer reflected in its dusky surface. I rose, went to kneel beside him.

"You see it?" I mouthed.

I felt his assent. He didn't reply.

We watched together, unspeaking, as the murkiness before us seemed to swirl languorously like smoke from a fire that couldn't quite catch.

She was coming.

My heart sped up with apprehension, but at the same time I felt great relief that whatever this was, Murdoch saw it too. I wasn't crazy. Not that I'd believed I was, more that I had suspected Murdoch was right about the effects of sleep deprivation. I could have dreamed what I'd seen earlier. Especially the small, shining light. It was pathetic how badly I wanted to believe in that spark within the darkness.

Then again, if I *was* losing it, I'd probably be the last to get the memo. People who should know seemed to believe that was how it worked.

"Is this all?" Murdoch asked in an undertone. "Is this all that happens?"

I shook my head. How would I know?

He put his hand out, and I grabbed his wrist. "No. Don't do that."

He looked at me. I don't suppose he could read my face in the indistinct light any better than I could read his.

I said, "I'm not sure what will happen if she touches you."

"She?"

We both caught the movement at the same instant, turning back to the mirror. There she was, floating beneath the silvery surface like a drowning victim in a cheesy horror film. Except there was nothing funny here.

She seemed dimmer now, further away, less distinct in form and feature. Granted, she hadn't exactly been solid to start with.

Murdoch sucked in a breath. "This is some crazy shit," he said softly.

I nodded.

We watched in silence. Yes, she was smaller, paler, more vaporous and insubstantial. Comparatively speaking. Because for an ordinary mirror, that thing was way too immediate and real for comfort.

"It's not going to grow fangs and jump out at us, is it?" Murdoch said. He was joking, but I could hear the unease in his voice. I could hear it my own when I replied.

"I don't know. I don't know what she wants."

"Did you try to communicate with it?"

"I don't know if you could call it that. She was laughing at me."

"Laughing?" He looked briefly from the mirror.

"She's not as — she was bigger before. More solid. I could see her more clearly. She could see me. She was laughing. Then she tried to put her hand through the mirror, like she was trying to find a way through." I could see the gleam of his eyes. "That's when I came to get you."

He grunted acknowledgement and turned back to the mirror, which was steadily growing more dim. "She's losing altitude fast," he commented.

I smiled. I liked his humor. Maybe it was just bravado, but it helped. "It must be almost daybreak."

"Yeah. My thought. Isn't that how it works with ghosts? They disappear at cockcrow?"

Murdoch had put it into words. One word. The word I had been trying to find a way around, a way past.

Ghost.

Along with all the rest of this junk I seemed to have acquired a ghost.

"If the campfire stories are right," I said. "I don't know. This is a new experience for me."

"I should hope."

We watched in silence as the diaphanous form grew fainter and fainter, and finally dispersed. By then, night was retreating from the edges of the room, fading to gray. It was not light yet, but it was no longer witching hour. The haunting was over for now.

I felt shaky with relief.

Murdoch also seemed to have concluded the danger was past. He sat back and scratched the back of his neck. "Wow. That was different."

I nodded.

He looked at me. It was light enough that I could now make out his features in the gloom. "What are you going to do?"

Good question. Call the Ghostbusters? An exorcist? The local news station? "I don't know. I'm not going to be sleeping here while I try to figure it out, though."

"No. I sure as shit wouldn't." He glanced at the mirror, which now reflected our two fatigued faces and bloodshot eyes. He climbed to his feet and stretched, arms over his head, muscles rippling beneath his furred chest. He yawned, displaying an impressive set of choppers. "You can crash at my pad for a few hours."

"Thank you," I said, and I didn't have to fake the gratitude. I had never felt as alone as I had this night. For a lot of reasons. It made me appreciate the simple kindness of one human offering another a few inches of space beneath his umbrella.

We didn't say anything on the weary trek downstairs to Murdoch's quarters. I was preoccupied with my thoughts, and I guess Murdoch was too. Sure, I'd watched *The X-Files* and *Buffy the Vampire Slayer*. Like everybody I grew up with, I was pretty open to the idea of the paranormal, but this was still seriously cray cray. Maybe I *was* sleeping. Maybe this whole thing was a dream and in a minute or two I was going to wake up on the grimy floor in a puddle of drool.

Next to me, Kirk kept giving those gargantuan yawns, so he must have been serious about needing his forty winks.

His rooms were a comfortable clutter of books and dirty dishes and assorted odds and ends. If there was a matching piece of furniture, it wasn't in view, but it was all good, solid stuff and built to last. There were two framed posters of Jules Verne book covers *The 500 Millions of the Begum* and *Twenty Thousand Leagues Under the Sea,* and a set of barbells. The infamous guitar was on a stand near the bookcase which was crammed with volumes, old and new. Sand dollars and shells filled a wooden bowl on a low coffee table the size of a raft. The long leather sofa was covered with newspapers.

Murdoch picked up the newspapers and dumped them on the half-buried coffee table. "I'll get you a blanket."

"Thanks." I sat down on the sofa, and then shifted. There was a CD case in the crack between the cushions. Linkin Park *Minutes to Midnight*.

Murdoch returned with what looked like a couple of wool army blankets. "So you inherited all that junk upstairs from the old man?"

"My Great-Uncle Winston. Yes. And there's probably half a million dollars worth of *junk* up there."

"I'll take your word for it. Is there some kind of record of where your great-uncle found all the different pieces in his collection?"

"Their provenance, you mean? Yeah. He kept pretty detailed records, but I don't recall seeing any notes like *haunted mirror*."

Murdoch snorted with what was apparently amusement. Or maybe the dust was getting to him. He tossed me the blankets. "Make yourself comfortable. Just don't wake me up before ten hundred hours."

"Huh?" That was some sleeping in he planned to do.

"Ten o'clock."

"Oh. Gotcha. You were in the army, right?"

He did a double take. "The *army*? Er...yeah. Sure. Sleep well. And if you can't sleep, don't get up and start pacing around."

I gave him a thumbs up — which was politer than my first thought.

He vanished down the hall and I heard a door close firmly. I shook out the blankets, which smelled of mothballs. I was still chilled. The heating here was mostly wishful thinking. Drafts whispered under every door and window, and the old radiator pipes banged and clanged like they were about to explode from the effort of warming this cavern.

I wrapped myself in the camphor-scented folds and then fished amongst the newspapers and periodicals on the coffee table for something to read.

Chris Pine grinned slyly from the cover of *OUT* magazine. I threw a guilty look at the silent hallway. Now *that* I hadn't seen coming. It was heartening though. I wasn't looking for a friend, but it was a relief to know there was no potential enemy here.

I flipped open the magazine and began to read.

Kirk didn't go in for lots of fancy gadgets or appliances. He had a vintage Faberware percolator, a machine for people who take their first cup of the day very seriously. I found coffee beans, a manual grinder which would have looked right at home in Great-Uncle Winston's museum, and made a pot of Sumatra.

It wasn't long after the dry rustic fragrance began to waft through the kitchen that I heard the creak of Kirk's bedroom door. He appeared in the kitchen a few seconds later clad in the same pair of faded jeans and a black and green plaid flannel shirt. His hair looked less like a raven's wing and more like a raven's nest. Did he stand on his head in bed?

"Hey, there you are," I greeted him. "And it's barely ten hundred oh thirty hours."

Kirk gave me a bleak look from beneath his black brows.

"It's snowing," I said. "Hard. How do you like your coffee?"

"Are you always this painfully cheerful?"

Now that really was funny. I laughed. "Well, you know how it is."

"No. I don't."

I said cheerfully, "Once you give into the darkness, it's hard to break free."

He growled, "I like darkness before my first cup of coffee."

I got two earthenware mugs from the cupboard. "You like darkness *in* your coffee or would you prefer cream and sugar?"

"Cream. Brown sugar. In the canister behind you."

I took mine black, but I found the sugar, got cream from the mostly empty fridge, doctored his coffee. Kirk accepted it with another of those uncommunicative grunts. He had squeezed into the breakfast nook and was staring gloomily out the narrow arched windows. The snow was forming white mounds at the bottom of the foggy glass, like an ant farm winter wonderland.

I scooted in across from him, taking my own mug in both hands. The coffee was hot and flavorful with a sort of earthy undertone.

Kirk stopped glowering at the weather, raised his mug, slurped noisily. He put the mug down. "Last night wasn't the first time you noticed something wrong with the mirror, was it?"

"Actually it was."

He started frowning again. "You didn't see anything before that?"

"No."

"How did it start? What did you notice first?"

"I'd been working all afternoon and I was taking a break —"

"Going for another stroll," he inserted grimly.

"And all at once I got this weird feeling of being watched."

Kirk said nothing.

"It was sort of unsettling because I couldn't shake the feeling. It went through my mind —"

"What went through your mind?" Kirk prompted when I came to an abrupt stop.

"It's going to sound crazy, but I wondered if there was some kind of peep hole or spy hole or something."

He looked taken aback. No wonder, since he'd have been the most likely suspect for your friendly, neighborly Peeping Tom. Not that my thoughts had been anything as coherent as a fully formed suspicion.

"Anyway, I had this sense of apprehension, of anxiety. It's hard to explain. It wasn't a rational feeling, but it was…strong. Really strong." I avoided his eyes. I could imagine what his expression would be like. "I was trying to talk myself through it and I happened to look at the mirror. Or maybe I saw something out of the corner of my eye. But there it was, this sort of filmy swirling." I put the mug down. Even now the memory of it made my hands a little shaky. "I kept thinking my eyes were playing tricks on me. That I was just tired."

I met Kirk's gaze then. His expression was grim but considering.

"So there I was, standing in front of the mirror, telling myself it wasn't happening, and," I took a deep breath, "it began to take form."

Kirk didn't say a word, didn't blink, didn't move a muscle.

"That was the first time. The second time, I mean after you came up and took a look and left again…"

"Go on."

"I thought I saw it reach through the glass." Kirk's face changed. I said hastily, "That is, I'm not one hundred percent sure because I was going for the door, but just for a second…it looked like fingertips stretched through."

"Holy shit," Kirk said sincerely.

A bell rang and we both jumped. Just like that the spell was broken. We both looked around for the source of that muted but insistent jangle. The doorbell? No, overhead. A phone was ringing.

I jumped up, nearly knocking over the table. "Damn. That's my phone!"

If he had a response, I didn't hear it. I was already out the door and on my way upstairs.

CHAPTER FOUR

There were only two possible callers, and I broke track records trying to get up the stairs before my not answering triggered the inevitable panic. I didn't make it in time.

"*Shit.*"

Chewing at a hangnail, I stood over the black rotary dial phone, waiting. Sure enough, the phone jangled again.

I snatched it off the cradle. "Flynn."

"*Flynn.*" I could hear the relief across the miles.

"Hi, Mom."

"Are you all right? Your voice sounds odd."

"I'm out of breath. I was downstairs. It's two flights."

"Oh. I'm sorry, honey. You didn't answer your cell phone."

"I left it up here. Upstairs."

"I suppose I should have left a message."

"That's okay. It's nice to talk to you." We both knew leaving a message wouldn't have solved a thing. She'd just keep calling until I actually picked up. Or she resorted to calling 911.

Mom asked tentatively, "How is it going?"

"There is a *lot* of stuff here."

"Yes, I suppose there is. According to Mr. McLennan, Winston ran that museum for fifty years. He just kept buying and buying and buying things for his exhibits."

"Yep," I said cheerfully. "Old Winston was a hoarder all right. This is going to keep me busy for quite a while."

"Well, that's good…"

"Yep."

"Are you sure it's not too much for you, though?"

"No way. This is what I need."

"The thing is, Flynn." Mom was proceeding with caution. I could hear the painstaking care with which she approached her real reason for calling. "Your father and I have been talking it over, and we just don't think you're ready for this."

I'd been expecting this, so I was ready. "Mom, you shouldn't say that to me. It hurts my confidence."

I heard her swallow, heard the little smack of her lips as she started to speak, but stopped herself. I gave her time, and she said, keeping her voice low so it wouldn't wobble, "We have an agreement, Flynn."

"I'm not forgetting. Have I ever broken a promise to you?"

"No."

"So everything's okay. I am keeping to my end of the agreement. Word of honor."

"Because if you were to go back on that, Flynn…" Her voice did break then.

"I know. Dirty pool." My mom's favorite euphemism for all nefarious and underhanded doings. "You're worrying about nothing. Really. I just need a little time to myself right now."

Poor Mom. I had her cornered. I was a horrible son. I heard the floorboards squeak behind me. I threw a quick, alarmed look over my shoulder, but it was Kirk. He was examining the mirror. I'd flown right past it in my haste to the get to the phone.

I refocused as my mother said, "It's just that you're so isolated there. Your father — we — worry about you being so much on your own right now. That building is practically in the middle of nowhere."

"Chester Connecticut is not the middle of nowhere. They have a farmer's market and a Chamber of Commerce and a cupcakery. Nothing says civilization like a cupcakery, right?"

"Yes, but you should be with people. People your own age. There's only that downstairs tenant and he sounds a little…"

"There *are* people my age around here." My gaze fell on Kirk who now leaned in the open doorway, listening to our phone conversation with some impatience. "Actually the guy downstairs is about my age."

"Math clearly not a strong point," Kirk muttered.

I ignored that, listening to her hopeful, "Oh?"

"And he's gay too."

Kirk's jaw dropped. "Excuse me?"

"Aren't you?" I asked.

"How the hell is that any of your business?"

"Is he?" I heard that note of cautious optimism and I winked at Kirk. If possible, he looked more offended.

"Yeah, he's kind of nice looking," I told her. "In an artistic, brooding, shaggy kind of way." I added, "Grooming clearly not a strong point."

Kirk scowled at me.

"Is he there?" my mother asked, and I probably should have felt guilty about the relief in her voice.

"Live and in person."

"What does he do?" my mother asked.

"He's a writer or something. Definitely not a musician."

Kirk opened his mouth but restrained himself.

"Oh, that's right. That's what Mr. McLennon said. He's a playwright."

"A playwright?" I marveled.

Kirk's face turned red.

"It sounds interesting," Mom said. "I don't think it pays very well, but he seems to be reliable about his rent."

"That's okay. We'll pawn some of the antiques and then I can keep him in the style to which he's clearly not accustomed."

She laughed almost sounding like her old self. "All right. Just keep records of your ill gotten gains for tax time."

"Will do."

"All right then. Oh. What's his name again?"

"Whose?"

"Your playwright."

"Kirk. Kirk Murdoch."

"Very Scottish!"

"Yep, he's a hoot, mon. Er, Mom."

She made a sound of patient amusement. "I'll let you go then."

"Okay. I'll —"

She broke in, "Flynn, you're remembering to eat and sleep and...everything?"

"Of course." I made sure she could hear the smile in my voice. "I'm better. Really. The work is interesting and that's what I need right now. And of course there's, um, Kirk."

"You're taking your meds?" Point blank this time.

"Yeah."

She exhaled, preparing to let go of the rope. "Your father sends his love. We both do. And you promise to call if things get on top of you?"

I looked at Kirk, opened my mouth, but that was probably taking it too far. "I promise. I love you, Mom. Love to Dad."

"Bye, Flynn."

"Bye-bye." I put the phone down and turned to Kirk. "So. How's our ghost this morning?"

Kirk looked pained. "Look," he said awkwardly. "Nothing personal. I'm sure you're a very nice guy –"

"Not really."

"— in your own weird way. But I'm not in the market."

I grinned. "Don't worry. That was strictly for my mother's benefit. I'm not in the market either. And even if I was, you're not my type."

He blinked. "Uh...okay."

"Any sign of You Know Who?"

"No. Everything looks normal." He glanced around the room, his gaze lighting on a mummified cat. "For this place."

"Perfect. I've been thinking of what to do about this situation, and I think I've come up with a solution."

"Let's hear it."

"I'll sell the mirror on eBay."

"You'll...?"

"Sell it. On eBay. I'll sell it *as* a haunted mirror, of course."

"Of course." He was looking at me like I was crazy. Granted, that was a look I got a lot these days.

"It's not as far out there as you're thinking. People sell all kinds of supposedly haunted crap on eBay. Mostly dolls. Old dolls are pretty creepy. And toys. I heard about someone putting her father's ghost up for auction. In fact, bottled ghosts have turned up a couple of times. And I remember seeing a haunted mirror sell a few months ago."

"For how much?"

"Not much. Maybe a hundred bucks. The point wouldn't be to make money, though. Although this is a valuable antique, and it's a shame to treat it like this."

"Is it? Then I guess smashing the glass and putting the frame in a wood chipper is out?"

I assumed he was kidding.

Kirk said, "If the point isn't to make money, why don't we just take the mirror to the Goodwill? Or the nearest dump?"

I was relieved he said *we*. Not that I couldn't deal with this on my own, but I appreciated having someone along to split the gas on my road trip to the Twilight Zone. "Maybe this is going to sound silly to you, but I don't want this thing going to someone not prepared to deal with it."

Kirk said slowly. "No, that doesn't sound silly to me."

"I feel like I've got a responsibility here. If some goofball wants to buy a ghost, that's totally different. That's on their head."

"I agree. But I don't think we should wait around for eBay. I think we should get the mirror out of here as soon as possible. Why don't you sell it to a local antique store? Tell them about the ghost. Human nature being what it is, and if this piece is as valuable as you seem to think, I'm guessing most places will be happy to take it off your hands for the right price."

I looked at him in surprise. That was a great idea. If I knew my fellow dealers, he was right about their willingness to take on the mirror, ghost and all. Plus I agreed with him about getting the mirror and its occupant out of the building as soon as possible.

"All right. I'll make some calls."

"I'll be downstairs. Let me know what you come up with. We can throw it in the back of my pickup and cart it off to wherever."

"Great. Thank you, Kirk."

He departed with a curt nod and a final wary glance at the mirror.

According to the web, there were eighty-six antique shops within a ten mile driving distance of Chester. Once I'd eliminated the clock repairs, the furniture restorations, the auctioneers, estate appraisers, the places only open by appointment, the places closed on Mondays, and the places taking a snow day, I was down to three contenders.

The grandmotherly voice at Lord Wellington's informed me they did not purchase items from anyone but their short list of qualified dealers, sonny, and in any case it was highly unlikely I had a genuine Regency ormolu mirror on my hands.

According to Poppycock and Peacocks, they had all the 18th Century mirrors they could handle, thanks very much.

Mystic Barne was interested. Very. But Mr. and Mrs. Barne were in danger of being snowed out if they didn't head home *right now*. So...maybe try them again tomorrow?

Five minutes later I was knock-knock-knocking on Kirk's door. He answered wearing perspiration soaked gray sweats and his usual scowl.

"It's no go," I told him. "We're stuck with the damn thing at least for tonight."

His scowl deepened. "I say we drop it in the trash bin out back for safe keeping."

I said apologetically, "It's easily worth about ten grand."

"You're kidding."

I shook my head. "This is kind of what I do."

"*Really?*"

"Well, not *this*, no. But I work for — used to work for — a dealer in Woodstock. New York, that is. I was only an apprentice, but he was going to make me a partner." Why was I sharing all that?

I could see Kirk wondering too. He said, "Okay. So it's valuable, but I thought you weren't worried about making money on the deal."

"I'm not. It's not just valuable because of how much it could be sold for. It's a piece of history. Guys were still fighting duels when this mirror was made. Jane Austen was writing *Pride and Prejudice*. Or one of those books."

"Jane Austen?" he repeated doubtfully.

"Yeah."

He shook his head. "Okay. Well, we don't want to upset Jane Austen. We've already got our share of peevish lady ghosts to deal with."

"And that's my other point. What if destroying the mirror doesn't get rid of her? What if it just frees her? Or majorly pisses her off? Or both?"

Kirk's frown deepened as he thought this over. "Why don't we wrap a sheet around it and put it in my truck. Pretty appropriate when you think about it."

"A mirror in your truck?"

"A sheet for a ghost."

"Oh right. Well, there's a basement in the building, right? We could stick it down there for the time being."

"The *basement*?"

"I know what you're thinking. *Don't go down to the basement!* But it would keep the mirror safe and keep it away from us."

"That's not what I was thinking." Kirk mopped his sweaty face on his sleeve, and nodded. "But okay. You want to lock it in the basement, I've got no objection."

"The only thing is, I've got dozens of keys upstairs, but nothing specifically marked basement. Do you happen to have one?"

He stopped drying his face and lowered his arm. "Have you not been down to the basement yet?"

"Not yet, no."

His mouth curved into an evil sort of smirk. "No? Well, hang on. I'll find a key. I want to be there to see your face when you open that door."

CHAPTER FIVE

It took Kirk about five minutes to find the basement key.

I waited in the entrance hall, staring out the tall mullioned windows and watching the snow drift down in lazy, silent swirls. It was coming down more heavily now. The leaden clouds had split open and miniature clouds were floating down, landing on sagging fence posts and peeling window sills.

If I closed my eyes I could remember snowflakes in Alan's eyelashes and his breath warm against my face…

"Found 'em," Kirk said cheerfully behind me. I turned and he dangled a couple of old fashioned keys on a key chain in front of my nose.

"So what's down there?" I asked. "Besides a decrepit washer and dryer."

"No washer and dryer," Kirk said. "And even if there was, I'd stick to using the Laundromat."

Laundry was something I probably ought to give some thought to. I would be down to my last clean pair of briefs any day now. Now *that* was scary.

"Afraid of the dark?" I asked.

"Afraid of spiders." Kirk's expression was bland. "Okay. Follow me. We'll see if we can make enough room down there to stuff in one more family heirloom."

A single flickering light bulb buzzed overhead as we headed down to the basement. The wooden stairway was narrow and steep, its steps designed for smaller feet than mine or Kirk's. The railing was loose.

"It's a lot colder down here," I said. Cold and cramped. The water stains on the walls and ceiling formed mysterious shapes, like the outlines of alien and dangerous continents on an ancient, fading map.

"Yeah, watch your step."

It wasn't going to be fun lugging that heavy old mirror down this gauntlet of rickety and unsafe stairs. And if we dropped it? What kind of bad luck could we expect? Would it solve our problem or unleash a worse one?

"So what is your type?" Kirk asked suddenly.

"Huh?"

"You said I'm not your type. What's your type?"

I thought of Alan.

"Gainfully employed for starters."

"Hey! I'm gainfully employed." He added, "I'm employed anyway."

"But you're not in the market."

"Very true."

I laughed.

We reached the bottom and Kirk led the way down a short and even darker hall, past some kind of a furnace room to another room with an ugly brown door. He fitted one of the keys into the old fashioned lock and turned it.

"Stand back."

I took a step back and he cautiously opened the door. Something heavy thumped against its surface, and I jumped. Kirk seemed to be expecting this, though. He craned his head around the edge and then threw the door the rest of the way open with the air of a magician yanking the drapes off a levitating lady.

My jaw dropped.

Kirk laughed.

It looked like the inside of one of those cartoon closets where the door opens to a landslide of tennis rackets and shoes and umbrellas and mousetraps and life preservers and Christmas ornaments and rubber duckies and everything else you could possibly imagine.

"What the hell is all that?" I asked faintly. I stepped back as a fancy white birdcage, perched unsafely atop a tall, narrow apothecary chest began to wobble. The whole wall of debris seemed to shift and start to slide. Kirk body slammed it back into place.

"That's some technique. You do that like you've had practice."

"Enough. You ain't seen nothing yet. This is just the tip of the iceberg. This landfill stretches all the way to the back wall."

"But where did all this come from? What the hell *is* it?"

"Everything your uncle didn't want upstairs. These are the things that *didn't* make the cut."

"Didn't he ever throw anything away?"

It was probably a rhetorical question, but Kirk answered, "Not that I ever noticed." He was smiling, seemingly pretty pleased with himself, so I must have looked suitably stricken as I absorbed the full extent of my inheritance.

I said, "From the way you were chortling to yourself, I was expecting a mummy case at least. Maybe an iron maiden."

"There's probably one in the back. I know there's a coffin in there somewhere because I helped the old man carry it in." Kirk's dark gaze held mockery.

"I…have no response to that."

"He was on the eccentric side, your uncle."

"I get that impression. I have no idea why he left all this to me. I never met him. No one in my immediate family did, as far as I know. Er…what just fell out?"

Kirk bent down and picked up a mannequin's head. He turned it to face me. The cold blue stare — that would be the mannequin's cold blue stare — looked back at me. "Alas, poor Yorick."

"He doesn't look like a Yorick to me. More like an Yves. I bet he got lost looking for his ascot."

"It's probably in there with his penny loafers."

I tore my gaze away from the glass eyes. "Shit. We aren't going to be able to fit anything else in this room."

"Sure we will. We just have to rearrange a few things."

"*Rearrange* a few things? We'd need a bulldozer."

"Nope. Just a plan and a willingness to execute it." Kirk cocked his head, studying the mountain of stuff. "We only have to make enough room to shove the mirror inside, right?"

"True. And it's only temporary."

"No sweat. I'll hand you the stuff and you stash it down the hall. We'll get this done."

We did get it done. It wasn't quite as easy as Kirk made it sound, but we managed to unload enough of the motley collection of furniture and boxes and assorted paraphernalia to make room for the mirror.

"We probably could have just left the mirror in one of the hallways," I admitted to Kirk as we climbed back up the stairs to my rooms.

"Maybe. But I'll feel more comfortable with her safely stowed away downstairs." He didn't seem to be kidding, which surprised me. I had the impression he wasn't easily spooked. In any sense of the word.

It was late afternoon by then, and the light, never great in that old ruin of a house — and especially not great on a gloomy winter's day — was failing fast. I felt a nervous sense of urgency that we get the mirror downstairs and locked in before dusk. It wasn't a logical feeling. It's not like the thing in the mirror was wearing a watch or had to punch a time card. It would appear, if it did appear again, whenever it chose. Assuming it had a choice in the matter.

"We should hurry," I said.

Kirk threw me a glance.

"Whatever it is, it doesn't happen in the daylight," I said. I did *not* want to be holding that mirror, trying to carry it down the staircase, the next time the apparition appeared.

Kirk must have followed my train of thought, because he nodded.

The assorted clocks were chiming the half hour as we reached the top level and I pushed open the door to my rooms.

The mirror reflected the pair of us looking a little worse for wear. Kirk had a smudge of dust across his left cheekbone and his dark hair looked wilder than ever. Next to him, I looked hollow eyed and a little on the spectral side. The feeble rays of sunset cast a bloody tint over us and the surrounding room.

From the bedroom, I could hear the cuckoo clock. I opened my mouth to make a joke and then remembered that it wasn't Alan with me.

It was strange and unsettling how for a few seconds I could forget that he was gone, that I was never going to turn and speak to him, laugh with him again. Recollection always came with a sickening jolt, like grabbing onto a live wire.

"Something wrong?" Kirk asked.

I shook my head, pointed at the next room. "Be right back."

I found a stack of stale-smelling sheets in the linen cupboard and grabbed a flat one, returning to the front room and Kirk. "We can cover the mirror with this." I draped a yellowed flat sheet over the mirror. I wasn't sure if it was an improvement or not. There was something a little too shroud-like about that large pale square.

"You take the base, I'll take the top," Kirk said, resting his large, square hands on each side of the arched top of the frame. Both ends of the frame were heavy and ornately carved with foliate scrolls and trelliswork. The upper frame consisted of almost a foot of arched cresting centered by a flower vase on a lambrequin and flanked by roses and angels.

I stooped, grabbed the bottom of the frame, and lifted. It was even heavier than I expected. Spots danced in front of my eyes.

"Got it?"

I grunted assent.

We lugged it out of the room, maneuvering it on its side to get it through the doorway, and then tottered slowly, slowly down the staircase with it.

Halfway down the stairway, Kirk signaled for a halt. We carefully lowered the mirror and leaned it against the railing.

"Jesus Christ, that's one heavy mother," Kirk swore.

"Yeah." And he was carrying the heavy end. "Maybe we could try sliding it down the steps?"

"You want to risk seven years bad luck with this thing?"

"We'd have to hang onto it, but maybe we could guide it down to the next flight?"

"Maybe we could ride it like a sled."

I grimaced.

We both looked down to the windows on the ground floor. My mouth dried as I saw the deepening twilight.

"I think this will be faster in the long run," Kirk said. He nodded at the mirror. "Her petticoat is showing."

The sheet had started to slip and I snatched it up, draping it once more over the curved top. It was probably childish, but I had a growing dread of what might be happening beneath the sheet. In all likelihood nothing was happening, but I couldn't be sure. I had a — probably superstitious — dread that now we knew about the mirror, our awareness would give the ghost strength.

We wrestled the mirror back up again and staggered unsteadily with it down the next stretch of stairs to the lower landing. There we wiped our sweaty hands and faces, readjusted our grips, and hurriedly lugged it the final leg to the ground floor. By then the twilight had melted into the darkness. Dark shadows thrust out in weird angles from the corners, slicing across the dusty floorboards.

The muscles of my shoulders and back were knotted with strain as we trundled our load across the hall. There were knots in my stomach too, but those came from escalating anxiety.

"We've still got to get this thing down to the basement."

"I know." Kirk was grim.

We started down the basement stairs. Kirk took the lead again, this time facing front gripping the sides of the frame to steady himself. The term "steady" was relative. I was pretty sure we were both going to plunge to our deaths. And while I wasn't particularly afraid for my own life, I didn't want to be the cause of Kirk's demise. I hung onto the mirror with all my strength and we stumbled down the last span of steps.

Despite the fact that the basement was colder than a meat locker, we were both flushed and heavily perspiring by the time we squeezed down the hallway and opened the door to the junk room.

My muscles shook as we levered the mirror upright. Even Kirk was breathing hard. We half scooted, half slid the mirror inside — by then I didn't care if we scraped off a grand or so of ormolu — leaning it back against the wall. I stepped into the hall, Kirk backed out after me, and slammed the door shut.

"You realize next we're going to have to drag this bastard *upstairs*?" I said.

Kirk nodded grimly.

We were silent as he turned the old fashioned key in the lock. As I heard the tumbler click over, I felt a sense of immense relief. Maybe Kirk did too because he let out a long breath and then glanced at me almost self consciously.

"Now maybe we can all get some sleep," he said.

"You do seem to appreciate a good night's rest."

"Damn straight."

That was the last thing either of us said as we climbed up the stairs again. As we reached the ground level, Kirk said, "Let me know when you figure out a new home for the Lady of Shalott. I'll be happy to drive her wherever she wants to go."

"The Lady of Who?"

"Tennyson. Never mind. I don't think they were teaching Tennyson when you were in school." Kirk peeled off, moving down the hall toward his rooms. "Just let me know when we can begin deportation. I'll be happy to clear my schedule."

"I'm hoping I found a buyer, but how fast we can move the mirror out of here probably depends on the snowstorm."

Kirk called without looking back, "Yep. Keep me posted."

I watched him go into his rooms. The door closed with finality behind him.

CHAPTER SIX

Muted and random guitar chords infiltrated the floorboards and insinuated their way into my consciousness. I put my pen down and rubbed my eyes.

The notes were too irregular and aimless to qualify as melody, and that was just as well. I couldn't listen to music anymore. Funny how a particular arrangement of flats, sharps and naturals could bring back a forgotten point in time, could recreate the way light fell across Alan's sleeping face, the scent of his aftershave, the sound of his laughter, the brush of his hand on my bare skin. Recall it all so immediately, so intensely that the return to present time felt like a punch to the heart.

Already his voice was starting to fade from my memory. How could that be when I'd known him all my life? When I'd spent more time talking to him than anyone else in the world.

I pinched the bridge of my nose hard. No good thinking of that now. That way lay madness. Literally, some would say. Lowering my hand, I stared blearily at the nearest clock, this one the green and gold Chinoiserie long case clock in the corner. Eleven forty-five.

That made nearly seven hours I'd been poring over Great-Uncle Winston's ledgers. And I had little enough to show for it. I'd been looking for some mention of the mirror, in fact, I was sure I'd seen a notation on it somewhere, but I couldn't find it now. Presumably my uncle had his own system of record keeping beyond scribbling every thought on any available scrap of paper. No, that wasn't fair. There were decades-worth of neatly filled in ledgers, but in the last years of his life, Uncle Winston seemed to have grown noticeably less meticulous.

A cocktail napkin that looked like an antique itself read: **Victrola Cab @1920. Carved finger pulls. No TT. Red face "on" indicator. 48"l x 48.5"h x 25"w.** There was a lot of that kind of thing.

Hell. Might as well call it a night. It was moot anyway. There was no offer anyone could make me for that mirror that was too low. At this point, I was willing to bribe someone to come and take the thing away.

I closed the ledger and pushed back my chair. A hot drink would be nice. An Irish coffee or cocoa laced with peppermint schnapps. But there was nothing like that in my uncle's cupboards, and even if there had been, I didn't treat myself to that kind of thing anymore. I had no time for self-indulgence.

Maybe I had more in common with old Winston than I thought, because he hadn't gone in for self-indulgence either. There were canned goods in his cupboards older than me, and if he'd bought a new set of sheets or towels in the last decade, they were safely hidden in a hope chest somewhere. No, if I really wanted to do myself a favor, I'd see if I could find a hot water bottle in that crowded, airless linen cupboard. The house was bitterly cold at night even when it hadn't been snowing off and on all day.

Somehow I couldn't get up enthusiasm for the hot water bottle hunt, though, and instead I went into the drafty little bathroom where, for the last forty years, Uncle Winston had shaved his whiskers, brushed his teeth, and watched his face grow older and older and older. I shivered. It was even colder in here. As frigid as though I'd left the window over the toilet standing open. I flicked the wall switch and one of the two bulbs overhead popped, leaving the small room bathed in a gray, dingy light.

"Great," I muttered. But maybe it was an improvement. In the poor light it wasn't as easy to see how badly the bathtub needed cleaning. The bathtub, the toilet, the fixtures, the mirror, me...

Yeah, even discounting the corpselike tint cast by the overhead light, I really did look terrible. I needed a bath, a shave, a couple of nights's sleep, and something to eat that didn't have the words "Fun Size" on the label. I needed to pull myself together.

Or I could just turn the gas on that antique stove in the kitchen up full blast and go to bed.

"Dirty pool," I chided myself, and popped open the medicine cabinet. I'd run out of toothpaste two days ago, but Uncle Winston had a lifetime supply of tooth-powder that tasted like a mix of dust and peppermint. Of course I could always amble downstairs and ask to borrow Kirk's. I pictured his reaction to yet another unannounced visit from yours truly, and sniggered.

Kirk. What was his story anyway? What was he doing living out in this run down and nearly deserted part of town? Talk about Off-Broadway. Why would anyone — anyone normal — choose to rent rooms from an eccentric old man in a death trap of an old house? Okay, the rent was ultra affordable. Even so.

Maybe his plays were so bad he had to hide out from the critics.

I shook some powder in my cupped palm, turned the taps on, and after a death rattle, icy water spurted out. I uncapped my toothbrush, the only genuinely clean thing in the room — maybe even the entire upstairs — and dipped the brush in the white-ish powder. Leaning against the sink, I gave my teeth a long, thoughtful sweeping.

Maybe I *would* sleep that night. All at once I was so tired I could barely stay on my feet. I scooped the frigid water up, swished it around my mouth, spat it out, splashed more cold water on my face for good measure, recapped my toothbrush, and replaced the powder in the cabinet. I swung the mirrored door shut.

I yelped and stumbled back from the sink. I wiped my eyes with my wet hand, peered through wet lashes.

"No way," I protested.

The surface of the mirror was nearly black, and rising through the inky blackness was an image. A face. No, not a face, exactly, more like a diluted and wavering reflection on water, or features seen through a mist. A miasma in this case, because those black and burning eyes and bared teeth belonged to something diseased, not sane, barely human.

"No, no, *no*." It *couldn't* be happening again. This time it *had* to be a nightmare.

The hazy image began to solidify, take form.

Kirk's door flew open on the third knock. Okay, given the speed with which I was hammering his door, it was more like the thirtieth knock, but that had to do with how fast *I* was moving, not how fast he was moving.

"I'm going to kill you," he announced, "and no jury in the world will convict me."

"It's not the mirror. It's upstairs."

"What's upstairs?"

"Upstairs is haunted. Not the mirror. The top floor of this house is haunted."

His head fell back and he groaned. It sounded heartfelt. Or maybe gutfelt. Either way, he plainly expressed pain in every anguished particle of out-rushed sound. "That's impossible."

"I know. I agree. But I'm telling you, she's up there. I just saw her in the bathroom mirror. I think it was her. Maybe not. Maybe it was another one."

Kirk raised his head and gawked at me. "What are you *talking* about?"

"Just now. I was getting ready for bed, and when I looked in the mirror there was something else there. I think it was her, but she didn't look the same. She looked...I don't know how to describe it. She looked...her eyes were black and dripping. She looked muddy, moss stained. You have to see it for yourself."

"Yeah, I can't wait to see that!"

"Kirk, you have to hurry."

"Christ Almighty. This is where I came in." His black brows drew together in a genuinely forbidding glare. "You know what I think, Flynn? I think *you're* the common denominator."

"Are you coming or not?"

"How is this my problem?" A flat statement of fact.

My heart seemed to drop like a water balloon hitting the pavement. "Oh. Well... true. Fair enough. It's not your problem."

I didn't have another plan though, so I continued to stand there like a wind-up toy one spring short of a full key-turn.

Kirk swore something passionate and uncomplimentary, brushed past me, and headed for the stairs. For the first time I noticed what he was wearing. Or rather, what he wasn't wearing, which was pretty much anything. Everything. Nothing. He wore black briefs. And that was all he wore.

And while I was never going to care about such things again, I couldn't help noticing that Kirk was put together very nicely. Wide shoulders, narrow hips, long legs. Everything in perfect proportion to everything else. He was made to move, made for action, briskly jogging up the stairs while I trailed behind.

It wasn't that I meant to trail behind. The heart was willing, but all at once I seemed to have run out of steam. Or adrenaline. Whichever it was that had kept me in motion for the past...however long it was now. Steam was probably as likely as anything else.

Ahead of me, Kirk reached the top landing and vanished inside my rooms. I grabbed the railing, hauling myself past the winking, leering faces carved into the banister. Were the expressions different now or was that my imagination?

As I gained the top floor, Kirk called, "You better get in here, Ambrose."

Ambrose again. He really was not happy with me. Well, that made it universal.

I found him in the bathroom inspecting the mirror which was now filled with nothing more sinister than Kirk's black scowl. His dour reflected gaze met mine.

"It's like before," I said. "If we turn off the lights and wait, I'm sure she'll show up."

He turned to face me. "Do you hear yourself?"

I listened to the mental echo. I said cautiously, "Yeah?"

"Really?"

"Well…yeah."

Kirk gazed ceilingward. But if he was looking for divine intervention it would have to come from the dead moths in the dirty globe of the overhead light because the other kind was asleep at the wheel. That I could guarantee.

"I see," he said with exaggerated patience. "So did you want to take the tub or the toilet?"

I glanced uncertainly at the now perfectly ordinary bathroom cabinet mirror. "I…"

"Yeah, me neither. I want you to listen to me and listen carefully, Flynn. This house is not haunted. Not the upstairs and not the downstairs. Do you think I wouldn't have noticed? I've lived here for two years. Your uncle would have mentioned a ghost. It's the mirror. If it's anything."

"If it's *anything*? What does that mean? You saw it yourself!"

He winced. But the next second he was glaring again. "Okay, so it's the mirror. Which is safely locked up downstairs."

I took a breath, trying to pitch my voice to a calm, reasonable decibel. "If it's not these rooms, then she's moving from mirror to mirror. I'm telling you I saw —"

"What did you see? You said you weren't sure it was her. You said maybe it was someone, some *thing* else."

"The point is, whatever it was, it was *there*. It was in the mirror. I didn't dream it!"

"Are you sure? When was the last time you slept?"

"There. Was. Something. There. Something…awful." My voice shook despite my effort at control. "I didn't dream it." My heart was racing. I was close to panic as I foresaw Kirk walking out of here and leaving me to whatever haunted this place. I'd be sleeping in my car before I spent the night in these rooms alone.

Maybe he saw how close I was to losing it, because Kirk sighed. "Flynn, listen to me. If you don't sleep, you'll crack up completely."

"Got it." I swallowed. "I need sleep. And probably a shower. My cracks are starting to show. I still saw something in the mirror. I didn't dream it. I'm not imagining things. I'm not hallucinating. I don't know why this is happening, but it *is* happening." I added, and maybe it was too close to pleading, but what did I have to lose really? "Kirk, you saw it. You know you did. There's something here. You know it."

He stared at me for a second or two with a kind of furious impatience. But then, astonishingly, he said, "Okay. There was something there. Locking her in the basement isn't enough. So tomorrow we get rid of the mirror. In the meantime…" I could hear the reluctance in his voice, "you can crash at my pad again."

I nodded, not trusting my voice.

When we reached his rooms, Kirk pointed to the sofa where the blankets I'd used the night before were still stacked. "You know where everything is."

"Yeah. Thanks."

"Same drill. Don't wake me before ten."

"Right."

He went down the hall, but then returned. "Do you want something to help you sleep?"

"What did you have in mind? A two-by-four over the head?"

"That's Plan B."

"What's Plan A?"

"Trazodone."

I wearily lowered myself to the sofa. "That's okay. I don't really do drugs."

"Shot of brandy?"

I shook out one of the blankets and draped it over myself picnic table style. "I think I'll sleep tonight, but thanks."

"Suit yourself." Kirk disappeared down the hall again.

I spread out the second blanket and lay for a few moments blinking sleepily up at the ceiling and wondering what was going on upstairs in my rooms. After a bit, I reached up and turned out the lamp.

"Maybe you have sleeping sickness," I greeted Kirk the next morning.

He snorted. "You think *I* have sleep issues?" He headed straight for the coffee pot. "Did you sleep in those clothes?"

I said in my best Southern belle accent, "Ah hadn't tihme to pack mah valise."

Kirk spluttered, coughed up coffee, then recovered enough to inquire, "Are you ever *not* bundled to your chin in a bulky sweater?"

"It's cold in this dungeon. I think we need a new furnace. Is the offer to use your truck to cart the mirror out of here still good?"

"Yep."

"Because the snow has stopped and I think we should get going while the getting is good."

Kirk raised his coffee mug to his mouth, slurped another thoughtful mouthful, and lowered it. "Okay. Suits me. Maybe we'll finally get some peace and quiet around here." He glanced at the clock over the breakfast nook. "I'll meet you in the basement in ten minutes."

"Synchronizing my watch now," I called on my way out the door.

I had a final look around for papers relating to the mirror, but I didn't expect to find anything, and in that I wasn't disappointed. I brushed my teeth — avoiding looking in the mirror — ran a wet comb through my hair, changed my gray sweater for my black sweater, grabbed my boots and parka, and ran downstairs in time to meet Kirk starting down to the basement.

The mirror was just as we had left it. We lifted it out of the basement and then began the long, arduous task of hauling it back up the rickety stairs. Luckily just one flight of stairs this time. Granted, it was probably the worst flight, given the narrowness and flimsiness of the steps. And we weren't racing against the clock this time. Even so, Kirk was out of breath by the time we reached the ground floor, and I had those black spots dancing before my eyes again.

We lugged the mirror onto the porch and propped it cautiously against a post. The cold air felt good on my flushed and sweating face.

"Wait here. I'll get my truck out of the shed," Kirk threw back as he went cautiously down the snow-caked steps. He disappeared around the corner of the building.

The snow swallowed the sound of his footsteps, swallowed all sound. It was a silent, white world I waited in. Now and then a non-existent breeze seemed to tease the bottom of the sheet over the mirror.

I could see the snow plow had already been down the lane that morning. That simplified everything.

"Lane" was an exaggeration. Pitch Pine Lane was really just a country road leading back into a small housing development. Way back. This house sat on the edge of the woods on the outskirts of Chester, and there was no other building or structure within immediate sight or sound. The house was formerly part of an estate, but most of the land had been sold off before Great-Uncle Winston bought the house. The lot the house currently sat on was large but unremarkable. The trees had all been cleared away and there were just a few scraggly shrubs, scattered sheds and fenced-in areas that looked more or less like trash dumps. A tilting telephone pole was loosely and dangerously tethered to the house by a stretch of sagging line. Kirk and I were probably the last people in the world with dial-up.

As for the house itself, it defied definition, architecturally speaking. It was kind of like an unhappy marriage of convenience between a demure Victorian cottage and a dissolute French chateau. Mottled ochre-colored stone and blood red rimmed windows and doors. The west wing was three stories tall and included an out-jutting windowless space that would have once been a green room or conservatory but now housed Kirk's truck. The east wing was four stories tall and capped by a crazy Queen Anne roof that looked like the sorting hat in Harry Potter, the one they slapped onto kids in order to determine which of the four school houses they'd been assigned to. Attached to the outer west wing were some low sheds with tin roofs, but they looked of more recent construction. I was using the closest as a garage.

I hugged myself, rubbed my arms. My teeth were chattering. In fact, now that I had time to think about it, I felt cold all the way through. Cold and sick. Was it some manifestation of the mirror? Like the pall of anxiety and fear that preceded the appearance of the apparition in the mirror?

More likely I was coming down with the flu.

Finally I heard the roar of an engine and a white Ford pick up drove across the blanketed lot in front of the house, winter tires chewing up the powder.

Kirk briskly backed up to the porch, jumped out and lowered the tailgate. "Watch your step," he warned as we levered up the heavy mirror.

He was right. The steps should have been shoveled or salted. I was a lousy landlord. It hadn't occurred to me that I had a responsibility here beyond sorting and sifting through junk. The snowplow had been down the main lane that morning, but our own drive needed a snow blower. Or maybe a bulldozer.

We slip slided our way across the porch and down the steps, managing not to kill ourselves or drop the mirror, which we loaded carefully into the bed of the truck.

Kirk raised the tailgate, locked it, and crunched around to the driver's side. I wiped my perspiring face, started for the passenger side, but the snow was deep, much deeper than I'd thought, and I seemed to be sinking down into it. Sinking deeper and deeper with each step, until the cold white blankness closed over my head.

CHAPTER SEVEN

"Flynn."

The voice was deep, quiet, calm. I liked the calm. I liked the quiet. I liked the fact that someone was there at the end of this long, long tunnel...

I opened my eyes. Blackened open beams. One of those mid-century — last century — starburst ceiling light shades. Gold stars on a black background.

"How are you doing?" the voice inquired, and I snapped back to the present.

I was lying on the sofa in Kirk's living room. Kirk sat on the coffee table, folded arms braced on his thighs as he scrutinized me.

"Hey," I said in a creaky, old man's voice.

His mouth quirked. "Had a nice nap?"

"I guess?" Had I? How long had I been out? I felt strange. Not bad. Not good exactly, unless it was the way you feel good after a bad hangover, when just not feeling horrendous seems wonderful.

I felt warm, that was the main thing — and the best thing. *Warmth.* God. When was the last time I'd been warm all the way through? It probably had something to do with the mountain of mothball-scented blankets piled on top of me. "What happened?"

Kirk cocked his head thoughtfully. "You have any health issues?"

I raised my head. "Me? No."

"Then I'm guessing it's not eating or sleeping for a week."

"I slept last night. And I had soup for dinner."

Kirk made a scornful sound. "You don't mean that Cup-a-Soup stuff?"

I felt compelled to defend Sir Lipton's honor. "That counts."

"Not really. Anyway, what happened is you blacked out. Then you sat up, spoke a few words of French, let me walk you in here, and had yourself a little..." He glanced up at the clock "twenty minute snooze."

"*French?* I don't speak French."

"Neither do I, so maybe it wasn't French. Anyway, you babbled something I couldn't understand, and then sacked out on the couch."

I sat up. "We've *got* to get that mirror out of here."

"Why? You think it's a portal to a Berlitz Learning Center?"

"I think whatever is wrong with that mirror is getting worse. Getting more powerful."

He grunted. "I see. This," he nodded at the cocoon of blankets, "is all because of the mirror. Because you were in such great shape before?"

"Well, I wasn't speaking French or having blackouts."

"Like I said, I'm not sure it was French. Maybe it was Portuguese. Maybe you just weren't enunciating very clearly. The point here is the dead faint and the fact that your core temperature felt like I dug you out of a snow bank."

"You kind of did, right? I was lying in the snow? Anyway, I feel okay now. I feel fine. I just want to get that mirror out of here." Actually, if I was honest, I felt like shit. Weak and shaky and wrung out, but I wanted that mirror gone. I wanted things back to normal. Or what passed for normal now. The new normal.

"Relax. We're getting the mirror out of here. But first you're going to drink this." Kirk held up a glass of green liquid, which I suspected he'd been hiding behind his back.

"What the hell is that?"

"Juice."

"*Juice?* God never intended juice to be that color. Juice is orange or pink. That looks like a beverage from *The Exorcist.*"

"This is exactly the color God intended juice to be." He handed it to me. "Drink it."

"You've got to be kidding. I'm liable to throw up just looking at it."

"Take it. Drink it."

The evil looking potion wasn't going away, so I took the glass from Kirk. "On your head be it. And that could be literally. Just sayin'."

"Drink it."

I held it up doubtfully. "What's in there?"

"Kale, spinach, celery, squash, parsley, spirulina, apples, oranges."

"That's not juice, that's soup."

"I hear you like soup, so just drink it and we can get going."

"Wouldn't two fingers of brandy be more traditional?"

"You're starving to death not having the vapors. Quit stalling and drink up."

I looked at the juice then looked at Kirk. I said uncertainly, "Why are you doing this?"

"I wish I knew, kid. Just drink the damn stuff. I want that mirror out of here as much as you do."

I doubted that, but I took a mouthful and swallowed. My insides did what felt like a belly flop on the sidewalk. "Ugh. Tastes like grass." After a fraught moment, the churning and bubbling in my gut died down and I expelled a cautious breath. "That's really awful."

"You're welcome."

"I'm not a kid, by the way."

"That comment right there is proof you're a kid." Kirk smiled. Probably the nicest smile I'd seen on his usually grim face. His teeth were white and perfectly straight, his eyes a warm gold-shot brown, like tortoiseshell. "You're what? Twenty-three? Twenty-four?"

"Twenty-six."

"You're a kid to me. I'm thirty-nine."

"Oh. Yeah, I see. Well, you're not *that* old," I said kindly.

He snorted. "Drink your juice, smartass."

I laughed and downed the rest of the witch's brew. It didn't get any better. I shuddered and wiped my mouth. "Does this work like Popeye's spinach? Are muscles going to pop out on my arms?"

He stood up. "I'll be content if you just pop out of those blankets and we can get a move on."

"I'm ready." I threw aside the blankets before I had time to think about how much I didn't want to see or touch that mirror again. "Let's do it."

Kirk tossed me my parka and I shrugged into it as we left his rooms and headed across the front hall. Our boots were by the front door, dripping onto spread open newspaper. It gave me a funny feeling to think of Kirk pulling off my boots and peeling me out of my coat. I must have been really out of it.

He opened the main doors and we walked out into the cold white world.

Kirk started down the steps, but checked mid-stride. I stopped too.

His truck was still backed up to the edge of the porch. A brown tarp to cushion and wrap the mirror lay crumpled in the bed. But the tarp was the only thing in the bed. The mirror was gone.

"You see that too, right?" I asked after a second or two.

Kirk swore and half ran, half skidded down the steps. "Look!" He pointed across the empty yard where four sets of deep footprints churned up the otherwise smooth spill of snow. Two pairs of boots. Four sets of tracks. Two people coming and going from the main road.

"No way," I said. "Someone carried it off? Someone *stole* it?" I wasn't sure if I was horrified or going to laugh.

Kirk's reaction was more straightforward. He was pissed, the black scowl back in full force. "I don't think it walked out of here on its own."

"How do we know? Maybe those are the mirror's footprints."

I was kidding, my normal inappropriate reaction to stress, but Kirk didn't hear me or at least didn't acknowledge he heard me. He stalked up and down the wavering line of prints, swearing quietly. And not so quietly.

"This is bizarre," I said. "Who the hell would even be out this way? Let alone have the balls to swipe something out of your truck. Especially something that heavy and hard to move?"

"Probably the same assholes who broke into the shed last month. And tried to break in the month before that. And the month before *that*."

Now there was an unwelcome news report. "Broke into the shed? Which shed? You mean like burglars? Were they trying to get in the house?"

Kirk nodded grimly, still studying the chunks of kicked up snow.

"They were *in* the house?"

He glanced at me. "No. They gave it their best shot. I discouraged them. Not enough, I guess." He added, "It's not a secret your uncle stored a valuable collection of antiques and art here."

"It just keeps getting better." I looked uneasily over my shoulder. Though weathered, the front door was heavy and well made. The handle and lock were another story. A good kick would probably take care of them both.

"You didn't report it?"

"Yeah, I did. To the cops and the property management company."

"The company didn't let my parents know."

"I don't know anything about that. I did my bit. Maybe they figured there was nothing to report. It's not the first try at a break-in and it won't be the last." He nodded at the footsteps disappearing down the lane. "We could try to go after them."

"Seriously?"

He shrugged at my tone. "Or not. Are you going to report this?"

"I think I should. Uncle Winston didn't keep enough insurance on the place, but there should be something. I don't want the mirror back, though."

"Don't worry," Kirk said dryly. "You won't get it back."

I absorbed this and my heart suddenly lightened. "So that's it. Problem solved. The mirror is gone."

"Looks like it." Kirk's gaze met mine and he gave a sour smile. "Try not to look quite so delighted when you talk to the law."

"Right." But I felt myself smiling for the first time in…well, I couldn't remember the last time I'd felt like smiling. Really smiling.

* * * * *

The Chester police force consisted of a Resident State Trooper. Portly and middle-aged Trooper Dunne showed up late that afternoon to take my report and, like Kirk, did not hold out much hope of recovering the mirror.

"Perfect timing for somebody, you leaving the item in question out there when you did," Dunne observed at last, putting his notepad away. He had big, bright blue eyes like a doll. They stared at me with as much warmth.

"Maybe they were in the area and checking to see whether the place was deserted because of the storm?"

"Maybe."

I thought I saw where he was going with this. "I don't even know if there's insurance on that mirror."

"Not saying you did," Dunne said. "Just saying it was convenient."

"There have been attempted break-ins out here before."

"Yep. And I guess there will be again. So don't go leaving any other valuables out where they could be grabbed by someone passing by."

"Trooper Dunne thinks I'm running an insurance scam," I informed Kirk a short while later. He had left the door to his quarters standing wide open while Trooper Dunne was in the house, so I figured even if it wasn't an actual invitation, he probably wouldn't mind an update.

"I'm surprised Trooper Dunne has that much imagination." Kirk was lifting what looked like an old-fashioned set of free weight barbells. A deep V of perspiration soaked his gray sweatshirt as he deliberately, methodically did his curls. His gaze was pinned on a spot past my right shoulder.

"I think it's really over. Something feels different. Lighter. Cleaner."

"Yeah?" Kirk exhaled a long, even breath, executing another slow, precise curl.

"Don't you think?"

He inhaled. His gaze veered briefly to my own. "Sure."

"Okay, that could be more convincing, but I'll take it as confirmation. Anyway, I thought you'd want to know."

Exhale. "Thanks."

I watched him for another moment or two. There was something both relaxing and pleasurable in seeing a perfectly made human machine functioning at such optimum levels of efficiency.

"I'll see you around," I said.

"Yep." Kirk inhaled.

* * * * *

It was over.

The fact that I finally found the reference to the mirror — purchased in 1956 at an estate sale in Louisiana — was moot. Interesting but moot. Because it was over.

REGENCY ORMOLU MIRROR WITH LATER CARTOUCHE-SHAPED PLATE, THE CONFORMING FRAME CAST WITH FOLIATE SCROLLS, STRAPWORK AND TRELLISWORK, THE ARCHED CRESTING CENTRED BY A FLOWER VASE ON A LAMBREQUIN, THE SIDES WITH CORNUCOPIAE, SCROLLED BASE, POSSIBLY FRENCH. $200. CASH.

I refolded the yellowed invoice back into its four fragile squares and tucked it back into the ledger it had fallen out of.

That night when I brushed my teeth, I risked a couple of cautious, sideways glances at the cabinet mirror. My own wide-eyed, foaming-mouthed reflection was all that met my gaze.

It. Was. Over. Whatever the hell it had been, it was someone else's problem now. And serve 'em right.

The next day I scrubbed the bathroom from top to bottom, using a gallon of bleach and giving the mirror several extra squirts of Windex.

Maybe Kirk couldn't feel the difference, but I could. Especially at night. Yes, I still turned around to look when the floorboards creaked, and I couldn't help thinking the hot water pipes clanked and clanged like they were possessed. I still occasionally had that weird sense that someone was watching me, but the heavy oppressive atmosphere was gone. At least the external heavy oppressive atmosphere. My internal atmosphere…climate controlled. Which was good enough. Nobody could ask for more than that.

Three days passed and I slowly but steadily worked my way through Uncle Winston's collection, identifying, appraising, cataloging.

I didn't see Kirk, which was fine with me. Now and then I heard his godawful, hopeless attempts at playing guitar; once in a while the smell of savory cooking infiltrated the floorboards. I liked knowing he was around, that I wasn't entirely by myself, but that was as much company as I required.

But on the fourth day he rose again. In a manner of speaking.

I was going through a stack of old books, checking and comparing editions on the Advanced Book Exchange, when a brisk and forceful rap on my front door nearly caused me to knock my chair over.

Kirk.

That surge of…well, it was relief. Relief because it was obviously Kirk knocking and not a supernatural manifestation. It was not pleasure, let alone anticipation. It was just relief.

I opened the door and caught him running his hands nervously through his hair. In fact, his hair was standing up in tufts as though I'd caught him pulling it out by the roots. His face jerked my way as the door swung open and he said with obvious relief, "You're here!"

"Hi. Yes. Where did you think I was?"

"I..." He looked so self-conscious and agitated that even I, not the most observant of others' feelings, couldn't help noticing.

"Is something wrong?"

"No. That is, I wasn't sure you were...up here. I didn't hear you."

"Huh? *Oh.* You'll be happy to know I've been sleeping the last few nights."

"You have? You *have.* That's good." *Definitely* a weird expression on Kirk's normally dour face. He continued to hover in my doorway looking sort of pained and sort of worried and very uncomfortable.

"Would you like to come in?" I asked politely, finally.

He startled me with an instant, "Sure."

I stepped back and he walked in, looking around as though he'd never seen these rooms before. Or maybe he was looking for something else.

"Is everything okay?" I asked again. "Would you like something to drink? I have water and Cup-a-Soup."

"Thanks. No. I'm..." Kirk seemed to steel himself to some unpleasant task. "Your mother called me."

My mouth fell open. "That was dirty pool," I said at last.

"She's concerned."

"But I just talked to her the day before yesterday," I protested.

"I know. She mentioned it. Anyway, when I didn't hear you up here, I thought maybe I ought to —"

"Check for the body?"

He was clearly not amused. I felt a stab of sympathy for poor Kirk. Plainly this was as excruciating for him as it was for me.

"I can imagine. Listen, don't take any of that too seriously," I said, hoping to make it easier on both of us. "My parents are a little overprotective."

He said awkwardly, but doggedly plowing ahead, "You had some kind of a breakdown?"

"That's kind of a dramatic way to put it."

"How would you put it?"

I shrugged. "The guy I planned on spending my life with died suddenly and, yes, I guess I had a sort of breakdown, if you want to look at it that way. I tried to kill myself. So that's all in the past, but obviously it was hard on my parents and they're still struggling with it a little."

I was trying to keep it light, but maybe I seemed a little too buoyant given that Kirk was gasping at the end of that speech. "You tried to kill yourself?"

"Weeeelllll, yeah, but it was really more of a cry for help." I'd figured he already knew that, but apparently not, and though I was trying to reassure him, he didn't look reassured. "I'm fine now." I put up a hand. "And before you say anything, just remember *you* saw the ghost too. I didn't make that up. I'm not crazy."

"I didn't say —"

"I hope that's true. To my mother, I mean. I hope you didn't say anything about what was happening here last week. You're just going to freak her out for no good reason."

"I did not say a word."

"Okay."

"Not least because I would sound as loony as you."

"I will take that as the compliment you clearly don't intend it to be."

Kirk suddenly laughed, surprising himself, I think.

"Anyway, I'm glad we had this little talk," I said. "But I probably should get back to work."

"Me too." Kirk hesitated. "But I was going to ask if you'd like to go grab something to eat tonight."

I stared at him, feeling the heat of embarrassment wash through my body. "Oh my God. Did she — she asked you to be my new best friend, didn't she?"

"No," Kirk said. "Thanks to you, she already thinks I *am* your new best friend. I was going to ask you out anyway. I mean, ask you to grab dinner. As your new best friend."

I couldn't help smirking at the care he was taking to not be misunderstood. "In that case, I accept," I said.

CHAPTER EIGHT

Not a date.

I reassured myself of this several times as the time drew near to start getting ready for dinner. No pressure. No expectations. A shower, a shave, and a swipe of deodorant. That was the extent of my preparations, and I'd have done that much for anyone.

I didn't want to go. I didn't want to have to try to make conversation — or, even worse, watch Kirk try to make conversation. I was sure it was something he would be very bad at. I didn't want to go to the trouble of pretending to eat. I didn't want to go to the trouble of pretending that I gave a damn. About anything.

I nearly cancelled. Twice. Okay, three times. But Kirk was now in contact with my parents, which meant a cancellation was liable to be reported, which would start the telegraph wires humming again. Might even precipitate a surprise visit from the parental units. No, I couldn't take a chance on that, so…dinner.

An hour or two at most.

Or maybe Kirk, having earned his good citizenship medal for the week, would forget all about it and I would be left in peace.

I dug out the cleanest of my sweaters, this one a bulky oatmeal cable knit. The nice thing about heavy sweaters was you could wear them a long time without having to wash them, but still. There was a limit. There were a lot of limits, actually. Since grooming was one of those things people watched for, I made sure to clean beneath my fingernails and behind my ears.

When five o'clock rolled around, I checked for my wallet, found my keys, grabbed my parka and walked downstairs to meet Kirk. He was locking his own door, and offered a polite, distracted smile.

I said, "You know when you showed up at my door this afternoon, at first I was thinking maybe you'd seen something."

"Seen something like what?" Kirk led the way across the scratched floorboards and faded carpet of the front hall. We paused to pull on our boots.

"Like *her*. You know, the lady in the mirror."

"Me? Why would she show up in my mirror?"

"Hey, I don't want to take that personally, but why not?"

"I don't think I'm her type."

I let that pass. "I can't help wondering what's happening with her right now, though. Do you think whoever stole the mirror, sold it? Broke it up for firewood? Has it hanging in their bedroom?"

Kirk gave a sour smile and quoted:

"Mirror, mirror on the truck

Where she went, who gives a fuck?"

I laughed as we stepped outside. It was dark, with a few early stars scattered across the indigo sky. The snow glimmered eerily around us. Kirk locked the door, and our footsteps, sounding hollow on the wooden planks of the porch, thudded down the salted stairs and were then swallowed by the snow.

"I found the original bill of sale. My uncle purchased it for two hundred bucks back in the fifties. From some estate in Louisiana."

Kirk grunted noncommittally.

After that I was out of polite chitchat. I glanced at Kirk's profile. He looked grave and thoughtful. A man on a mission. A mission of mercy, I guess, and clearly not something he was used to. I smiled inwardly at the thought of my parents tapping someone as anti-social as Kirk to keep an eye on me.

"Something funny?" he asked suddenly.

"No."

"You've got that foxy smile again. Like someone just handed you the key to the hen house."

"Foxy Loxy, that's me."

Kirk laughed. We reached his truck, parked in the former conservatory on the far side of the house. He unlocked the passenger side door and opened it. I climbed in, feeling self-conscious. It was the having the door opened for me bit. Alan and I had never bothered. Wouldn't have thought of it, and not just because we had automatic door locks.

Kirk walked around and unlocked his own door. He started the engine, letting it idle for a while, the defroster blasting out hot air over our legs.

Once upon a time I'd had lots of friends. But my friends were also Alan's friends, and somehow I couldn't bear to be around them anymore now that Alan was gone. It wasn't anyone's fault. They had tried, some of them had tried very hard to stay in touch. But I just couldn't do it. I couldn't talk about Alan with them — yet I couldn't think of anything else we had in common now.

Kirk had never known Alan, which made it easier. And he hadn't known me before, so he couldn't compare the old me with the surviving wreckage. I found that relaxing. No pressure to be "sweet, sensitive, funny" Flynn. Kirk had never known me to be anything but weird. A smartass weirdo. It was nice.

"How long have you lived here?" I asked as Kirk put the truck in motion and we started out across the white lot. Had he told me this before? Probably.

"Not quite two years."

"Did you know my uncle well?"

"No. He kept to himself."

"Which suited you fine."

"Yep."

I smiled faintly.

Kirk glanced at me and said, "Once in a while Winston would invite me up for a glass of brandy or loan me a book. And once in a while he'd ask me to help him cart something down to the basement or up from the basement. He was an eccentric, but he was a nice old guy. I liked him."

"Did you ever visit the museum?"

"No. He'd closed it up before I ever moved to Chester. The building is still there in Deep River between Bridge and Spring Streets. It's empty, boarded up, but it's still standing."

"It seems like a weird place for a museum."

"It was a weird museum, I guess."

"True."

We neither of us spoke again until we were seated inside the restaurant. Restaurant L&E was an "authentic" French restaurant on Main Street. The upstairs offered rooftop garden seating in summer, and a rustic Provencal farmhouse dining room in winter.

Kirk and I ate downstairs in the bistro, which was more casual and comfortable and not-a-date suitable. I ordered a bowl of French onion soup and a glass of red wine. The waitress apologetically carded me, to Kirk's amusement. Kirk ordered the Steak Frites, peppered hanger steak, fried potatoes, roasted shallots, watercress salad with blue cheese and wild mushrooms, and a bottle of pinot noir.

"Man does not live by juice alone," I commented as the waitress moved away.

"He could if he had to." Kirk shook out his napkin and placed it over his lap. For some reason that struck me as funny, but there was no reason Kirk shouldn't have good table manners. He knew his way around a wine list, for sure.

He asked, "So how long have you been in the antiques business?"

"Officially? Three years. I used to help out summers at Old Mill Antiques when I was a kid. I guess I kind of had a knack for the business. Anyway, I liked it a lot, so Mr. Gardener took me on as his apprentice when I got out of college." I really didn't want to think about that time now. Sometimes I felt stupid for not having known that that kind of happiness couldn't last, was only temporary at best.

For the first time I wondered how Mr. Gardener was doing. He was getting up there in years and he had relied on me more and more. I hoped he was doing okay. I hoped he'd found someone reliable to take my place.

The waitress arrived with our wine. I sipped my glass while Kirk went through the routine of sniffing the cork and tasting. He nodded, totally serious about the whole procedure, and the waitress poured him a glass.

As the waitress withdrew, I said, "Anyway, it's boring talking about myself. What about you? You're a writer?"

"Playwright."

"Have you had anything published?"

"Produced, you mean? Yeah. One of my plays was produced Off-Broadway. It ran for a whole three nights."

"That's amazing." Kirk's lip curled, and I said, "I'm serious. I bet almost no one ever has a play produced."

He made a huffy kind of sound, not quite a laugh, not quite a snort. "That's one way of looking at it."

"What way do you look at it? Your play only ran three nights?"

"That's what it amounts to."

"I think it's amazing. I've never known a playwright." I smiled at him. "How come you don't live in New York? Wouldn't that be a better place for a playwright?"

"Connecticut is practically the home of summer theater. There are plenty of working playwrights here. There's the Eugene O'Neil Theater, Long Warf, Yale Rep. Hell, Good Speed Opera House is right up the road."

"I didn't know that."

He shrugged. "If I could live anywhere, I'd live in Los Angeles. There's a growing revival of interest in the theater, plus you've got some of the finest actors and directors in the country permanently located there. Production costs are a fraction of what they are in most theater cities."

"Yeah, but the theater is just a novelty there, right? It's all about Hollywood and the movies."

"There are some top notch playwrights earning a living on the West Coast. Plus, there's the beach. I mean the Pacific Ocean."

"Oh, well there you go. What you really want is to be a surfer. You just don't want to admit it." I was teasing, but I realized I didn't like the idea of Kirk leaving for California. Well, good tenants were hard to find. I hoped that California was a dream and not a plan. "So what was your play about?"

"I...it was about Afghanistan. The war." He said it a little defensively. There was a tinge of pink along the sharp ridge of his cheekbones. "It was called *Act of War*."

"You were in Afghanistan? In the army?"

He nodded. Then said reluctantly, "Yeah. Well, I was with the Rangers. 1st Battalion, 75th Ranger Regiment."

"Rangers? You mean like black ops stuff?"

Kirk's eyes narrowed, his mouth thinned. "You're thinking Special Forces."

"They aren't the same thing?"

"No." He added, "I don't like talking about myself either."

"Got it." I took another mouthful of wine. "Anyway, lovely weather we're having." The wine was maybe not a wise idea given that I was already feeling its effect. It had been a long time since I'd let myself have a drink. Not because I'd ever had a problem with alcohol, but because alcohol made it too easy to forget — which made the remembering all the harder.

Kirk had been glowering at me, but at the "lovely weather" comment his upper lip curled into an unwilling smile.

We sipped our wine and then our meals were delivered. The soup was so good I was almost sorry I hadn't ordered a full meal.

"Are you writing anything now?" I inquired.

"Right now I'm just taking notes."

"Ha."

He neatly carved off a slice of steak. "How long do you plan on staying at the house? Do you know? Or are you here for good?"

"Ten months."

"Ten months? You're very exact. Not…almost a year? Not nine months?"

"Ten."

"Okay. Ten months." Kirk glanced up from his plate and smiled faintly. "It should be an interesting ten months."

"I'll do my best."

When we returned to the house on Pitch Pine Lane, a single light burned in the upstairs window.

Kirk said, "Did you —?"

"I did, yeah."

I felt his almost imperceptible relaxing, and thought I knew the reason. "I keep waiting for the mirror to turn up again."

"I can't imagine that." But Kirk fell silent too as we crossed the snowy yard and drew near to the darkened porch.

The porch was empty, of course, and we said our goodnights in the downstairs hall and went our separate ways.

I felt pretty good, even a little smug, about getting through my dinner out with Kirk. I had made it through an entire social engagement no worse for wear, and if Kirk was in contact with my parents, he'd be able to honestly report that I was eating, drinking, and accepting invitations. That let us both off the hook.

So it was disconcerting, in fact irritating as hell, when the very next day my cell phone rang and it was Dr. Thorpe suggesting an impromptu get-together.

"Mark and I are on our way to Montreal. We were hoping you might be free for dinner." Dr. Thorpe's voice was deep and melodious, and his soft Virginia accent sounded like the Shenandoah Valley and home. But I did not want to see him. I did not want to have dinner with him or his partner Mark — although I appreciated Dr. Thorpe's attempt to make it sound like a genuine social occasion and not the mandatory request for my presence that we both knew it was.

"Sure!" I said brightly. "It'll be nice to see someone from home."

I could hear the smile in Dr. Thorpe's voice as we finalized the details. When I hung up I put my head in my hands and howled. "*Goddamn* it. Why the shit can't people leave me *alone*? I don't *want* dinner. I don't want to *talk* to anyone. Why does everyone keep *interfering*?"

First Kirk. Now Dr. Thorpe. What next? My parents? Dr. Kirsch? What the hell was the *matter* with people?

I spent the rest of the day worrying about the evening to come. What would Dr. Thorpe expect to see? What would happen if he didn't see what he expected to see? I nearly started biting my nails again, but *that* would be a tell tale sign.

By late afternoon I had worked myself into full blown anxiety. I showered, shaved, and headed out to Essex to buy new jeans and a new sweater so that I could be sure I looked presentable.

Kirk's door was closed as I crossed the front hall.

My car was in the larger shed on the opposite side of the house from where Kirk stored his truck. I wasn't sure if it had formerly served as a gardening shed or a byre for animals. As I unlocked the door and stepped into the darkness, I smelled the faint odor of chemicals and what was hopefully dung and not human excrement.

I opened the door and slid behind the wheel. The last time I'd driven anywhere was when I had arrived nearly two weeks ago. The interior of the car smelled ever so faintly of Alan's aftershave, though that was probably my imagination. It had been months since the last time Alan sat in my car. In fact, I didn't remember the last time, and for a few minutes I couldn't move, racking my brain, trying to remember. I didn't want to forget a single moment.

Had we gone grocery shopping? To his parents' house for dinner? A movie? Why couldn't I remember?

This was how it started, bits of memories chipped away by time and distance till there was nothing left.

I *had* to remember.

My hands grew damp on the steering wheel. I closed my eyes tightly and tried to visualize…yes, there it was. I had picked him up from work and we had gone out for Indian food. I'd had Chicken Rasam and Alan had Chettinad Chicken. He always loved the really hot and spicy dishes. And he'd talked about his promotion to Station Manager. But of course the promotion had never happened because two weeks later Alan was dead.

I let out a long shuddering sigh, wiped my eyes. I turned the key in the ignition. It was okay. I still remembered everything.

CHAPTER NINE

I opted for skinny jeans and a bulky navy blue pullover with a shawl collar. I couldn't hide how much weight I'd lost, so the best strategy seemed to be to make it look like a fashion statement. Depressed people didn't worry about how they looked, therefore trendy jeans and an expensive sweater argued that I was on an even keel. Even stylin'.

From the shop in Essex I drove straight to Restaurant L&E — Dr. Thorpe's suggestion — and had a glass of wine in the downstairs bar to fortify myself for the evening ahead.

It wasn't that I didn't like Dr. Thorpe. I liked him a lot. I owed him a lot. If it hadn't been for Dr. Thorpe's intervention, I'd still be sitting in Silver Springs Psychiatric Hospital talking to Dr. Kirsch and getting electroshocked when he didn't like the answers.

Dr. Thorpe was the one who pointed out that if I was determined to kill myself, no one could stop me. Dr. Thorpe was also the one who had come up with The Agreement. And I suppose that was the reason he felt like he needed to make sure I was okay now.

Which I was.

I sipped my wine and stared out the etched windows at the sleety rain and deepening twilight. Eventually I saw Dr. Thorpe's tall figure walk past. Another man, younger, slighter, darker, was with him. The door to the bistro opened and I finished off my wine.

When I glanced up again, Dr. Thorpe and Mark were making their way over to me. I stood up, smiling.

"Flynn," Dr. Thorpe said warmly. He put a hand on my shoulder, a compromise gesture somewhere between a hug and a handshake. "You remember Mark?"

I sort of remembered Mark. They hadn't been together that long. He was English. Probably in his thirties. He had a thin, intelligent face with weirdly intense dark eyes and a cynical curve to his mouth. His accent sounded like he should be introducing *Masterpiece Theater.*

"Sure. Hi, Mark," I said, offering my hand.

"Hello, Flynn," Mark said. *Beginning tonight on* Masterpiece Theater. *It's not enough that Stephen and Mark must interrupt their much needed holiday, first they must dine with Stephen's barmy patient. I bloody well hope these barbarians serve a decent spotted dick!*

"Did you have trouble finding the place?" I inquired.

"No trouble," Dr. Thorpe said, glancing around the crowded room. "This is nice. You said you'd been here before. How's the food?"

Tick tock, back and forth, tick tock, back and forth.

Eventually we were upstairs, seated in the crowded, rustic style dining room with linen covered tables loaded with white china and gleaming silver and starred candles. "I think you should probably call me Stephen," Dr. Thorpe was saying.

I smiled. "Okay, Stephen."

Dr. Thorpe didn't usher me into the world, but he was the first doctor I really remembered. He saw me through chicken pox and having my tonsils out and the time I broke my arm wrestling with Kenny Pinney. I'd always thought he was handsome for an old man, but I realized now he must have been a very young doctor when my mother had first taken me to see him. Although his hair was silver and had been for years, he looked like he was only in his forties. I'd been to his fiftieth birthday party though, so I knew he was older. He had very green eyes and a warm smile. A kind smile.

He had tried to be kind when he had to tell me about Alan. I could remember every line in his face. He had looked terrible. His eyes had been black and his face white. He had been Alan's doctor forever too. Alan even had a little crush on him. I wondered if Dr. Thorpe ever knew that?

"I am not losing both of those boys," Dr. Thorpe had said to my mother the night I came home from Silver Springs. "We're not going to lose Flynn."

I'd sat in the shadows of the hall staircase and listened to Dr. Thorpe and my parents talking quietly in the front room, making their plans, plotting my future.

"I'll have the Steak Frites," I told the waiter.

That's bistro menu only," he apologized. "I can recommend the Steak Au Poivre."

"That sounds great."

Mark ordered another bottle of Côtes du Rhône, the waiter faded into the mass of tables and candlelight, and Dr. Thorpe said, "I don't think we've let you get a word in edgewise, Flynn. How's the cataloging coming along?"

"It's a bigger job than I expected. And a lot dustier." We all laughed.

"Your uncle used to own a museum? What kind of things did he collect?" Mark asked.

"It was called the Museum of the Arcane. He collected all kinds of freaky things. I found a box of shrunken heads the other day. I think they were for real. And there's a mummified cat and an antique ghost detector."

"What every home needs." Something about Mark's accent made everything sound sarcastic. Of course, he probably *was* being sarcastic that time.

"But there's also a lot of ordinary stuff. Limoges china and art deco silver, alabaster lamps and a cuckoo clock. Lots of clocks. That probably means something, but I don't know what."

"What happened to the museum?"

"I guess my uncle closed it when he got too old to run it. I'm not sure really. He wasn't in contact much with the rest of the family, and he died while I was in Silver Springs." I glanced at Dr. Thorpe. He was watching me with a grave attention that made me unhappily aware that we were not three friends casually getting together for dinner, however hard he and Mark were trying to make it seem that way.

"Anyway, the work is fascinating. There's a fortune in furnishings alone in that old house." My thoughts shied away from the memory of the mirror.

"You're not nervous there on your own?"

I don't think I'd have caught it, except Mark gave Dr. Thorpe a lazy sort of look. Dr. Thorpe appeared instantly self-conscious. So I knew the look had been a warning and they had already checked out the house on Pitch Pine Lane.

I smiled cheerfully. "I'm not on my own."

"That's right," Dr. Thorpe said. "Your mother mentioned there's a tenant staying there as well?"

I nodded, reaching for my wine glass. I resisted the temptation to drain the entire thing in a gulp.

They waited politely for me to fill in the blanks. I couldn't really think of anything to say. I wanted to ask if they believed in ghosts, but I knew what they would make of that. I'd probably be back in the booby hatch before the pots de crème were served.

"He plays the guitar very badly. I can hear him at night sometimes."

Dr. Thorpe chuckled.

This encouraged me to say, "He's a playwright. He was in Afghanistan. In the war."

"Was he?" Mark asked, suddenly on alert.

"Mark spent time in Kandahar." Dr. Thorpe looked at Mark, and Mark looked at Dr. Thorpe. No need for words, no need for anything but each other. I knew that look. I knew that understanding. That's how it had been between Alan and me.

Our dinners arrived and the spell was broken. I left the conversation to Dr. Thorpe and Mark and made myself cram in every bite of food I could, faking a hunger I hadn't felt in months. I don't know what they talked about, I didn't care. I smiled and nodded and answered when I had to and tried not to look at the hour hands on their watches, which didn't seem to be moving anyway.

Just after dessert was served, Dr. Thorpe's cell phone rang. He checked it and rose. "I'm sorry. I have to take this." He smiled apologetically at me and eyed Mark. It was a different sort of look from the earlier one.

I watched him thread his way through the tables and then I glanced at Mark. His thin mouth curved in a funny, wry smile.

He said in that lazy, elegant accent, "Stephen's afraid I'm about to tell you what I am going to tell you."

I asked uneasily, "What are you going to tell me?"

"Only…you're not wrong, you're not mad, for feeling as you do. If something happened to Stephen, I'd feel the same. I'd probably make the same decision you did."

"Uh…thank you." No wonder Dr. Thorpe was worried. I could feel a bubble of laughter filling my chest and rising up in my throat. I was afraid it would burst out of me any second.

"But it would be a mistake. Certainly for someone as young as you."

"Yes. I get that a lot."

Apparently Mark didn't have much sense of humor. It was impossible to tear my gaze away from his unnervingly bright scrutiny. "You'll have to take my word for this, but I've spent a great deal of time around the dying and the dead. I do know about being bereaved and what I can promise you is, if you'll hold on, give yourself sufficient time, you'll be all right. I don't say you'll get over it. I don't believe you will, but you'll learn to be happy again. You'll even learn to love again. If you'll permit yourself."

Any desire to laugh was gone. "No. I won't. Not ever."

"Perhaps not. But the pain does ease, Flynn. Humans are meant to survive and be happy. All one really has to do is hang on long enough."

"Well, thank you, Mark," I said tersely. "I appreciate the advice."

"No, you don't. Naturally you don't." He smiled with unexpected charm, glanced past me and said, "And here's Stephen come to rescue you."

I smiled brightly at Dr. Thorpe and devoted myself to choking down the rest of my dessert. I'm sure there was more small talk. Probably coffee. I don't remember any of it. I made my escape as soon as I could.

All I could think on the short drive back to Pitch Pine Lane was what a horrible mistake dinner had been. Despite the craziness of the past two weeks, or maybe because of it, I had started to feel almost normal again. Well, maybe normal was too strong a word, but now, in the space of a few hours, I was back to despair. And it wasn't Mark's misplaced if kindly-meant advice or the knowledge that I hadn't had any choice in going to dinner or that my parents were petitioning people to keep an eye on me. It wasn't any of that, though those were all good reasons for feeling depressed. No, it was seeing Dr. Thorpe with Mark, seeing how comfortable they were, how well they understood each other, how much they loved each other.

I didn't begrudge them their happiness, but it was unbearable to watch.

Right now Mark would be confessing to Stephen that he had butted in and done exactly what Stephen had told him not to do, and Stephen would be yelling at Mark — well, that was unlikely, impossible to imagine really, but Stephen would be voicing his disapproval in that soft Virginia accent that sounded so much like home, like my dad, like Alan...and later in their hotel they would make up their argument and lie in each other's arms and talk quietly until one of them fell asleep. And the other would hold him, and his heart would be filled with contentment and a foolish belief that the world was a safe and good place.

The rain had stopped again. The street lamps grew small in my rear view mirror and then melted into darkness. There were only the white beams of the headlights to illuminate the empty road unrolling ahead.

I felt sick. Too much food and too much wine.

It was a short drive but it felt like forever before I turned off on Pitch Pine and drove on to the empty lot at the end of the lane. The lights were all off in the house. It looked abandoned in the pallid light cast by the crescent moon, crooked and mis-shapen like a magical house in a folktale.

I parked in the shed, crunched across the slushy snow to the front porch and started up the steps, only to recoil at the vision of someone walking out of the darkness toward me.

But no. It wasn't someone. It was me. It was my reflection.

The mirror stood at the top of the stairs.

I watched myself stumble back and land at the bottom of the steps. The black glass showed only me, none of the yard. No trees, no stars, no snow. Just me framed in a swirling black void.

Move. Don't let it see you.

I got up, watched myself weaving, gaping within the confines of the gold ornate frame. That crushing sense of dread was back, a disturbing presentiment pressing in from all sides.

Something horrible was going to happen.

That was animal instinct, not reason; but all the same, I sidestepped, took myself out of the box created by the frame. I stared wildly around the blanched yard.

Now what? What was I going to do?

I could leave. I could jump in my car and drive to a hotel. In the morning I could come back and finish what Kirk and I had started to do before the mirror had been stolen.

Kirk.

He was still in the house.

Well, but that was okay. He was safe inside the house, right? He was the one who'd said the mirror didn't want him. He could take care of himself.

All these thoughts rushed through my brain, but most clearly was *Go. Go while you can. Get away from here.*

But I couldn't. I couldn't just leave Kirk sleeping with this thing sitting right outside his door.

I didn't have the courage to edge past the mirror on the porch. I had a clear memory of that pale hand reaching through the glass. No damned way was I putting myself in arm's reach. I felt my pockets for my keys. There was a back entrance to the house, and a door through the conservatory where Kirk kept his truck.

I turned and started across the mushy snow, looking through the tall, frost-crackled windows along the side of the house. I had been wrong. There was a light on inside the house. The chandelier in the main hall offered a feeble, dusty radiation not strong enough to dispel the shadows — in fact, it only served to highlight them.

My footsteps shushed through the snow. The moon slid back into the clouds and the yard and its surroundings grayed out.

I glanced through the next panel of windows and saw someone staring out at me. A dark figure stood in the entrance hall. Not Kirk. I saw that at once. The figure was too small. Too still. It was a woman. A woman in an old fashioned black dress, her face shrouded by a black lace mantilla.

My Irish grandmother used to talk about the banshees and say their cries could make your "blood run cold." For the first time I understood what that meant, what that felt like. She was out of the mirror. She was free. She could walk right into Kirk's room.

Who knew what she could — would — do?

I ran, my feet sliding and slipping, sinking into the snow. I lumbered around the corner of the house and began to bang on the window of what I believed must be Kirk's rooms. Particles of ice dusted down where I beat the glass, stinging my face.

"Kirk! Kirk, it's me! Kirk, wake up!"

It went through my mind that Kirk, being ex-military, might have a gun, might even shoot me by accident. Or maybe not by accident, given how he felt about having his sleep disturbed. I kept pounding, but nothing happened.

I gave up, stumbling to the next window, thumping my fist so hard I thought I would shatter the glass. "Kirk! For God's sake! Wake up!"

The windows were dark. I couldn't remember if he had blinds or drapes, but whatever was across the glass formed an impenetrable barrier.

"*Kirk!*"

The darkness fluttered wildly and slid away. A pale form filled the window. The next moment, the window sash scraped up with a shriek to wake the dead — as if they weren't already up and making house calls. Kirk leaned out. He rasped, "You gotta be shitting me."

"The mirror is back. She's in the house," I gasped. "You have to get out."

"You lunatic. Do you have *any* goddamned idea of the goddamned time?"

"Listen to me. *She's in the house.* She's right outside your door. You have to get out now. While there's still time!"

CHAPTER TEN

I didn't think Kirk heard, let alone understood me, but mid-tirade his tone changed and he lunged forward. "Give me your hand!"

I thought he wanted help climbing down, but his fingers clamped around mine and in that very different voice he said, "Get up here."

"What? No. You're not listening. She's *in* the house. Now. Right now."

"*Flynn*. Move your ass."

"Kirk —"

He was looking past me. Even in the gloom, the expression on his features alarmed me. His other hand locked in my collar and he roughly dragged me toward him. "You just don't get it," he panted.

I got it then and I quit arguing and scrambled up and over the sill.

I spilled onto the floor, and Kirk slammed the window shut. I rolled over and stared at him. He was watching the window with as weird an expression as I could imagine ever seeing on his craggy face. I turned to the window. At first I couldn't see anything, nothing to make Kirk look like that. But then my vision sharpened.

A shadow pressed against the glass. Indistinct, formless, no more substantial than a black mist...but it was there. A shadow that somehow cast a pale, unnatural glow as the apparition took form.

Brass rings jangled as Kirk yanked the drapes shut, cutting off my view, breaking the spell. His words were flat, almost shockingly prosaic. "That bitch gets a better signal than my cell phone."

I said faintly, "She was right behind me."

"Yeah."

He turned on a lamp. I sat up, still staring at the drapes. A chill rippled down my spine, my scalp tingled with revulsion. Was she still out there? If we pulled the curtains back would we see a black veiled woman floating in front of the window? Or was she gone? What stopped her from floating right through the wall? Ghosts could do that. Doors, windows, walls…none of those mattered to a ghost. I'd read plenty of *Goosebumps*. I knew these things.

I glanced at Kirk. He was still scowling at the window. He looked more angry than frightened. Angry and thoughtful.

"How do you know she's not coming in here after us?" I asked.

"I've ringed my rooms in salt." He said it tersely.

"I'm…did I hear you say you rang — ringed — your rooms in salt?"

"Yeah." Kirk directed his scowl my way. "Sea salt. I've been reading up on this stuff. Ghosts. Hauntings. Salt is considered the most effective barrier. Sage works too. I used sage as well as salt in the living room. I figured that was the most likely point of entry."

I opened my mouth, started to speak, started to speak again, and finally gave up and settled for staring at Kirk. He stared back at me. His hands were braced on his hips — once again he was not wearing anything more than black briefs. Nice to be impervious to cold. And ghosts. The soft lamplight illuminated a wrought iron bed with rumpled sheets and blankets, a couple of chests of drawers, and a large brown painting of a solitary house in the middle of barren hills.

He said slowly, "You really thought *I* needed rescuing?"

"Hell yeah, I thought you needed rescuing! She was standing right there, right outside your door. How did you know that mirror was going to be returned? Why didn't you tell me?"

"I didn't know the mirror would be returned. How would I know that? I just figured if Winston brought one haunted piece of furniture into this place, maybe he brought other things that might be a problem."

Kirk was so matter-of-fact about it, I didn't know what to say. It had never occurred to me there might be more than one haunted artifact in my uncle's possession. Although maybe it should have, given old Winston had been running a museum devoted to "the arcane."

"Do you think she's gone now?"

"Probably. Do you want me to look?"

"No."

He gave a short laugh. "See, that's the problem right there."

I pushed wearily to my feet. It had already been a long night. "What's that? What's the problem? Other than the obvious problem, I mean."

He said with that old bluntness, "Your fear. Your fear is the problem. *You* are the problem. You're the catalyst. You're the trigger for all this spooky bullshit."

I didn't think I could have heard him right. But his face was dark and fierce with emotion. Anger probably, and as Kirk's words sank in, as I absorbed that he was serious, my own temper blazed to meet it. "Excuse me? How do you work that out?"

He pointed at the window like it was too obvious to need explaining.

The nice thing about anger was it really didn't leave much room for fright. And it had a pleasant warming effect, too. "You're for real? *I'm* causing this? Me? *Me?* I'm the problem here?"

"The facts speak for themselves. I've lived here for two years, just about, and nothing like this happened until you showed up."

"I don't believe this. That's it? That's your proof *I'm* to blame? It never happened before?" I couldn't get my head around it. How could he say these things to me? Not only was he talking total illogical shit, this was so unfair. I could have jumped in my car and driven away the minute I saw that mirror sitting on the porch, but no. Idiotically, I had imagined Kirk might need help, at least a warning.

Getting ambushed by someone who I had stupidly started to consider a friend left me reeling.

"I didn't say you were to *blame*," Kirk said in a now perfectly reasonable tone. "I said you're the catalyst. The conduit. I told you, I've been reading up on this. You're open to this negative energy, to psychic manifestation. Your depression, your grief feed —"

"Oh, fuck you, Murdoch," I managed to get out, my voice shaking. I turned, but unexpected tears blinded me so that I walked right into a chest of drawers. I heard a clatter like a wooden bowl full of horse hooves hitting the floor, and I stepped over whatever I'd knocked off the top of the chest. Sand, no, that would be salt, crunched underfoot as I finally found the glass knob of the bedroom door. I turned the knob, got the door open, and started across the obstacle course of his living room.

"Flynn, wait a minute." Kirk's hand closed on my shoulder. I tried to throw him off, but he hung on. "Stop. I'm not saying that to — it's not a criticism. Exactly. We've got to figure this out. That's all I'm saying."

"You figure it out. You've got all the answers." I tried to free myself again, but his grip tightened on my shoulders, his large, warm, capable hands holding me in place.

"Hear me out."

"I've heard plenty already. You're right. I am depressed. I am grieving. I am scared —" I stopped before I had to add "humiliated" to the list. One thing I was not, was in the mood for grappling with a mostly naked guy. True, it was a little warmer downstairs, but why the hell did he have to keep parading around without clothes on? And why the hell did he have to keep standing there, holding me in a grip that was both hard and kind, gazing down at me so solemnly. Warm, male, alive.

"You coming to warn me just now? That took guts. I know that. And I know you're not afraid of dying. So what is it you *are* afraid of? **What is it you think this ghost, this specter can do to you? That's what we have to figure out. Once we work that out —"**

"You don't know what the hell you're talking about!" This time I did free myself. Or maybe Kirk let me go before we got into a wrestling match.

He didn't say anything, just continued to frown at me, black brows in a straight line, but I was beginning to know his frowns and his scowls, and although I didn't want to see it, didn't want to recognize it, there was concern there. Concern for me.

It brought the tears back to my eyes, closed my throat, made my sinuses burn. I didn't want to feel this, didn't want to feel anything. Not even anger. It had been an exhausting evening. Harrowing. Made worse by the reminder that people were worried about me, cared about me, refused to let go of me.

Refused to let me let go.

I shook my head. Kirk said quietly, "Whatever you think, I am your friend. Let me help you, Flynn."

"You can't help me." I drew a deep, shaky breath. "See, that's the thing. I don't need anyone's help. And as far as what I'm afraid of? I don't know. I don't know how to —" Tears spilled from my eyes, running into my mouth. I had to stop and wipe my face on my jacket sleeve. "I didn't believe…there was anything after. I didn't believe in heaven or…I sure as hell didn't believe in ghosts or anything like that. I didn't believe. But now I know…there is something. And Alan is out there, part of that… and I don't know if I'm going to see him again or not. If she can stop me…if she can change what happens for me and Alan." My voice cracked on Alan's name.

I hadn't cried when Alan died. It wasn't shock or numbness. People had that wrong and kept making a big point of my lack of tears, trying to say it was denial or refusal to accept. It wasn't that at all. There was too much feeling to get out. Too much feeling to leak out through my eyes or nose, let alone form coherent words. It was a tidal wave building and building and building. There was no way to funnel that. Release meant annihilation. I knew that, even if they didn't, and now there was no holding it back.

It broke out of me in a coughed sob. I struggled to get breath, lungs expanding, but another of those sobs wrenched out, half strangling me. And then another. It felt like my chest was convulsing, ripping apart. I didn't remember how to cry. The more I fought it, the more it hurt.

I didn't even know what I was crying for. Alan? Me? Uncle Winston and his little shop of horrors? Kirk emptying boxes of salt on hardwood floors?

There wasn't any stopping it, it was coming like a flash flood of rocks and boulders and sand, knocking me to my knees. Somehow Kirk was there, holding me in powerful, warm arms, keeping my head above water while those sounds tore from me, rending the silence of the room, the house, the night.

He didn't say anything. Or if he did, it was drowned out by the roar in my head.

I don't know how long it went on, but finally there was nothing left, not a drop, not a hiccup, nothing left but the occasional exhausted shudder. Kirk was still crouched, still supporting me, cradling my head on his shoulder. All at once I was so tired I could have closed my eyes and gone right to sleep. I felt wrung out, unsubstantial. And yet somehow not empty, not hollow in the same way I had been before.

Peace? I wasn't sure what that was. But something inside me had changed, relaxed, slipped free.

Kirk got me to my feet, and it was a relief that he didn't try to talk to me, didn't say a word, just guided me to the sofa, helped me out of my jacket, out of my boots, helped me lie back against the cushions. He piled those mothball scented blankets on me — they were starting to smell familiar, even comforting. The only light came from the open bedroom door and the darkness was soothing and restful.

I closed my eyes.

* * * * *

I woke to a sound like the Crack of Doom.

I tried to pry my eyes open.

Earthquake? Tornado? Demolition Derby?

No.

Snoring.

The kind of snoring probably not heard since the last woolly mammoth entered the deep freeze.

I sat up, dislodging what appeared to be a couple of small silver balls, which jingled merrily down the sweep of olive brown blankets till they hit the floor and, still tinkling with holiday cheer, rolled away under the coffee table.

Kirk, sprawled uncomfortably in a tangerine-hued "easy chair" that looked anything but easy, sat up with a snort. He peered at me through the gloom.

"Er, sorry. I think I was sleeping on your jingle bells," I said.

He cleared his throat a couple of times and got out a scratchy, "You okay?"

"Disappointed Santa didn't bring me a fire engine. Otherwise fine."

Kirk didn't say anything, and some quality in his silence, raised prickles of unease on the back of my neck.

"And how are you?" I asked politely.

"Fine."

"What time is it?" I shoved the blankets back and another silver ball rolled down the slide of bedding, it's jingle muffled by the folds. "What the heck?" I found my cell phone. 11:57.

"It's practically noon!" I told Kirk. "I slept twelve hours."

"Monday."

"Sorry?" I began to think the trouble I was having reading Kirk's expression had nothing to do with the poor light.

"It's noon on Monday. You've been sleeping — mostly — for thirty-six hours."

"*What?*"

"Check the date on your phone."

After a moment, I looked down at the screen on my phone. Monday, February 13, 11:58. "That's weird. I haven't been sleeping more than a couple of hours at a time."

Yeah. It was a lot weirder than oversleeping. That was more like a coma. Or catatonia. Or the first day of summer vacation.

Kirk tossed aside the blanket he'd been using, and rose. I saw that he was dressed in jeans and a corduroy shirt.

"I don't understand." I knew from the way he was acting there was something more at work here than me oversleeping. Mostly I was grateful that whatever had happened, he hadn't phoned my parents.

"Let's go get something to eat."

"Go out?"

"Yeah. Let's go get breakfast."

"Well...but wait a minute. I have to shower. I have to brush my teeth." My mouth felt like a moldy carpet and I urgently had to pee. "Is the mirror — where's the mirror?"

"The mirror's in the shed on the east wing, wrapped in a tarp. Not that it makes any difference."

I was getting more confused by the moment. "How did you move it by yourself?"

"Using the tarp and a rope tied to my truck."

"Okay," I said slowly. "Just let me wash up and change my clothes."

"You can wash up down here."

"Now you're starting to weird me out."

"I think it's better if we stick together."

A cold sinking feeling washed through me. "Look, I know I was — I know I lost it last — Saturday night. But I'm okay. I'm not going to jump out a window or anything. Really." Now I was worried that maybe he *had* reported my breakdown to my parents. Were they on their way to Connecticut? Was Dr. Kirsch going to show up any second with his trusty hypodermic needle?

Kirk was shaking his head. "This isn't anything to do with that. At least, not directly. I hope. Either way, I think we need to get off the premises where we can talk freely."

I opened my mouth, closed it. Opened it again to say, "All at once I feel better. You sound crazier than me."

"If you're going to wash, go wash. We don't have a lot of time."

I wasn't in the shower long enough for the water to heat, and I made do with rubbing toothpaste over my teeth with my finger. Kirk was tossing his keys impatiently when I left the bathroom.

I followed him out to his truck. When we were on our way, I said, "I guess I need to let Trooper Dunne know the mirror has been returned."

Kirk gave one of those uncommunicative grunts.

"Will you still help me take that mirror over to Mystic Barne this afternoon?"

"I'm not sure it's going to be that easy."

"Because whoever stole it brought it back?"

He said grimly, "That's got to factor into our plans."

I was glad he said "our." "Plans" didn't come amiss either.

I said, "We were fine all the time the mirror was gone. That must mean it has a limited range."

"It looks that way, but we could be wrong about that. We don't know anything for sure. Except that it seems to be getting stronger."

"It," I said thoughtfully, watching the pretty shop windows of Chester slide by.

"I don't know what you want to call it. Entity? Apparition? Whatever it is that uses that mirror as its home base."

"I've always read these descriptions of haunted inns and castles, and they always made them sound sort of cute and cozy. Like it would be no problem to coexist with a lost spirit. But this thing is nothing like that. It's angry and..."

"Dangerous," Kirk agreed. He looked away from the road. "You feel that too?"

I nodded. "Antique or no antique, maybe destroying the mirror *is* the only answer."

"I don't think the physical destruction of the mirror is going to get us anywhere. And at least this way we have a focal point for her. If she's just free floating out there, that might make everything worse."

"She can get out of the mirror now."

"She may not be able to move far from it, though."

"She can move from mirror to mirror. We know that for sure. Of course if we destroy the mirror she might take up residence in the bathroom cabinet."

He snorted. "When the mirror was gone we didn't have any problem."

"True. But the mirror didn't stay gone. If we knew who she was, maybe we could figure out what she wants."

"Maybe she doesn't want anything anyone could give her. Maybe the only thing she wants is to cause harm."

"So what are you thinking? An exorcism?"

"In ghost hunting circles it's called a cleansing."

I tried to laugh, but it wasn't very funny.

We had breakfast sandwiches at The Villager on Main Street. I was surprised to find I was actually hungry. Starving in fact. The coffee was hot and strong, and the egg and cheese and tomato on fresh baked bread tasted like the best thing I'd ever had. I ate every bite. Kirk ate two sandwiches.

Sitting in the cozy, charming café surrounded by antique signs, historic black and white photos, faded wooden crates, it seemed crazy to be talking about ghosts and, well, evil. But evil was what we were really faced with, wasn't it?

I stared at the large sepia-toned mural of woods and a giant castle. I said, "I'm no expert on this stuff, obviously, but in the movies the only way to get rid of a ghost is to figure out why it's still hanging around. Maybe I need to go back to the beginning."

Kirk's dark brows drew together in that stern line. "Go back to the beginning how?"

"I know where my uncle purchased the mirror. A plantation called Bellehaven somewhere in Baton Rouge. Maybe I need to...I don't know? Maybe I should go down there. See what I can learn."

He stared intently at me. "No. In fact, this is what I was going to tell you. You have to leave. You have to go home to Virginia."

"Huh?"

"You have to leave. When we get back to the house, you have to pack your stuff and go."

He didn't seem to be kidding. In fact, he was about as sincere as I'd seen him. He actually looked sort of regretful.

I said kindly, "Kirk, I'm technically the landlord. So if anyone has to leave, it would be you. Not that I want you to leave, unless you want to take the mirror with you, in which case you have my blessing."

He got out his cell phone and began pressing buttons. "You can't stay, Flynn. It's not safe for you."

"That's *so* sweet," I said shortly. "But I'm sta —" I broke off as Kirk held his phone up to show me a grainy video on the small screen. I leaned forward for a better look, trying to hear the blurred video.

I felt an unnerving shift, as though the air pressure had changed, as though a trap door had opened. The bottom had just dropped out of the only reality I knew. The lighting was terrible, but even so, I could see the video was of me. I was sitting on Kirk's sofa and I was speaking quietly, venomously. Quietly, venomously in French.

CHAPTER ELEVEN

"That was you last night," Kirk said. In case I missed the point.

It took me a second or two, but I got out, "It turns out I don't like having my sleep disturbed either." Neither of us laughed.

I couldn't tear my gaze away from the mini video. Off screen, another voice, Kirk's, was calmly questioning the onscreen me. "What is it you want? Why are you here? Can you speak English?"

The onscreen me seemed to wind down, speaking more slowly, sleepily. My scalp crawled, listening.

Real life Kirk said gruffly, "Do you see now?"

"I see I missed an easy A when I didn't take French as a high school elective." I answered automatically, my brain going a million miles a minute while I tried to make sense of what I was watching on the small screen.

Possession? Was that what this was? I was possessed by a ghost? A French lady ghost at that? Was she somewhere inside me at that very instant? Or was she just renting space in the evenings? It was unbelievable. I was the most ordinary person I knew. But fuzzy though it was, that small image was unmistakably me.

"I know you don't want to hear it, but I guess because of your loss, you're more receptive to whatever this is. A spirit, a ghost, an entity...you are vulnerable to it."

I appreciated that he was trying to be more tactful than the first time he'd suggested I was the catalyst, but I had to point out, "How do we know? Nobody's watching you sleep. Maybe the same thing is happening to you when you're counting Zzzzs."

Clearly the idea had never occurred to Kirk. The scowl returned full force. "That's not very likely." He turned off his phone, which was a relief.

"I'd have said the same thing, but you're holding the proof in your hand. Speaking of which, if that video ever makes it onto YouTube, I guarantee to personally haunt you to the end of your days."

"You need to take this seriously, Flynn. I don't scare easy, but you scared the shit out of me last night."

I could believe that. I felt pretty shaken too. I was very grateful he hadn't called my parents or 911 when I'd conked out. Either time. "Okay. So you think the solution is I run home to Virginia and you deal with the mirror? How do you plan on doing that?"

"I haven't worked out the details. I was thinking maybe of putting it in cold storage on the other side of the state for the next fifty years."

"I thought we were being serious."

"Seems practical to me. We've speculated that this spook has a limited range. So we isolate her — it — from humans."

"Fine. If that's the solution, I'll take care of it myself and then I can get back to work cataloging Uncle Winston's collection."

"I don't think that's a good idea."

"And that would be because why?"

"Because we don't know what else is up there. Or down there. Because we don't know for sure that our lady in black is restricted to the mirror's location. Because the risk to you does not justify the gamble."

"What do you care about the risk to me?" I scoffed. "A hard ass ex-Ranger like you? No way. You just want your isolation chamber back."

"That's true. I can't get anything done with you around. You're one distraction after another. Interruption, I mean. But also —" He stopped as though recalling himself.

"Also what?"

He sighed. "Also I promised your father that no harm would come to you in that house. Not on my watch."

"You…" I wasn't sure if I was offended or simply flabbergasted. "You promised my — when? When was this?"

"Friday morning. He phoned me."

"My *dad* phoned you?" But come to think of it, of course. *Of course* my parents were not going to take it for granted all was well. They weren't built like that. Dad was ex-military intelligence and Mom was a lawyer who donated her free time to a battered women's shelter. They were neither of them the sit-back-and-wait-to-see-how-things-developed type, and they already blamed themselves for not seeing the "warning signs" last November.

"One army man to another?"

Kirk gave me a wary look. "Sure."

"So…nothing personal. You promised my parents you wouldn't let me stick my head in the oven. It's not like we're actually friends."

"I don't have friends."

Whatever you think, I am your friend. Well, people said things in the heat of the moment. I smiled, though smiling was the last thing I felt like. "That must simplify your life."

Astonishingly, Kirk looked ceilingward. His face worked as though he were in pain. At last, he looked directly at me. "Of course we're friends. I don't know how and I don't know why, because the last thing I need or want is involvement with another human. Especially a human carrying as much baggage as you. But yeah, we're friends. Which is why I want you to go. As soon as possible."

I had no clue what to say to that. I could see he was dead serious. I chose my words carefully. "Believe it or not, I feel better than I have in months. That was the best sleep I've had. If I dreamed, I don't remember it. And I'm hungry. I can eat. I feel halfway normal again."

"You feeling rested and refreshed after a bout of ghostly possession isn't exactly reassuring news."

"It isn't necessarily bad news." I didn't have to force a smile this time. "Look, Kirk. You're not responsible for me. That's one of the good things about friendship. I'm not going to ask you for anything more than the occasional use of your sofa or your truck."

He glowered.

"In fact, I'm going to give you what you want. Partly, anyway. I'm going to give you some space. I'm going to Louisiana. I made my mind up while we've been talking. I think the only way to resolve this is go back to the beginning."

Kirk's frown gave way to surprise. "I thought you said that mirror was over a century old. You think you're going to find someone alive who can answer your questions?"

"I don't know. It makes sense to me that the only way you end a haunting is by figuring out what's keeping the ghost stuck on the, er, mortal plain. At least that's how it works in all those movies and books."

"What are your parents going to say about that?"

"I'm not actually under house arrest." I wasn't, right? A feeling of unease flickered at the back of my mind. The topic of me traveling around the country had never arisen, for obvious reasons. I hadn't been in a touristy frame of mind when I'd left the hospital. "I'm twenty-six. It's not like I haven't been making my own decisions for years."

"I'm just asking."

"It's a non-issue."

"Sure. Are you independently wealthy or something? Because you seem to have a lot of money for someone your age."

"I am, yeah." Kirk's questions were hitting a nerve. Alan and I were pretty good at saving plus I did have a trust fund, not to mention all of Uncle Winston's dubious assets. I'd never had to worry about money, but one of the problems in being committed to a psychiatric hospital for any length of time is you lose complete control of your life. And when you try to resume that life, everything from having a license to drive to being able to vote ultimately becomes someone else's — or even the court's — decision. Technically, my parents were once again my legal guardians. My finances had never been discussed, and as far as I could tell, nothing had changed. That didn't mean they couldn't yank my wallet out of my hands if they decided there was a problem.

"Must be nice."

"Do you think you could forward that video of last night to my phone? I want to see if I can find someone to translate." I recited my number.

Kirk typed the number into his cell and pressed send. "Done. When are you leaving?"

"This evening." I was already checking flight information on my phone. "I'm booking my flight now."

"Book two seats," Kirk said. "I'm coming with you."

I looked up, startled. "What? That's crazy. Listen, I've traveled a lot. I enjoy it. I like flying. And I'll be hundreds of miles away from the mirror." But even as I said it, I couldn't deny that I liked the idea of Kirk coming along. Two heads were better than one, especially when neither head knew what it was doing. Kirk might be many things, most of which I had no inkling, but he was sure as hell capable.

"Maybe so, but I'm still coming with you." He gave me a bleak look. "In case you never noticed in all those movies and books, it's the ghosts that usually win."

* * * * *

It was raining when we touched down in Baton Rouge. A light spring rain glittered the tarmac and mottled the glass and concrete terminal buildings, bringing out the sharp smells of dust and tar and a bite of sulfur. The night air felt warm and moist, despite the fact that it was February and we had left Connecticut blanketed in white and looking like a Christmas card.

We collected our luggage and rental car, and were on the road to St. Francisville by eleven-thirty. I drove. The four lanes of Highway 61 were mostly empty that time of night. It was a short drive, a little over half an hour. The windshield wipers kept lazy time, beating out the gently rising and falling miles of ancient oak trees, glimpses of silvery ribbons of river, and moonlit antebellum plantations.

We didn't talk much. The GPS had a southern accent which provided a couple of laughs. We'd spoken equally little on the flight. Kirk had ordered a couple of whisky sours, read a few pages of *America's Master Playwrights* by Stella Adler, and then napped. He slept lightly though, waking himself up each time he started to snore.

I was glad he wasn't in a chatty frame of mind. Not that I could really picture Kirk in a chatty frame of mind. But I was particularly grateful for his terseness now. Glad for a break from what felt like the emotional marathon of the last few days. I realized one of the things I liked best about Kirk was how quiet he was, how stoic. He reminded me a little of Alan in that. Alan had been quiet. Not stoic, but gentle. Kirk wasn't gentle. Not that I'd noticed, but even when he was yelling, it felt mostly impersonal. I found myself wondering about his comment about not wanting or needing involvement. Not romance, not relationships, *involvement*. It seemed like a crucial difference.

For the first time in a very long time I was curious, actively wondering about a fellow human being.

That was when I wasn't busy wondering about how to begin my investigation of the lady in black. I already knew that Bellehaven was no longer a private home. It was a museum open nine to five daily. The chances of finding a handy aged family retainer were small to none. But I had to start somewhere.

"Have you ever been down this way?" I asked, finally breaking the silence.

"No," Kirk answered at once. "I spent some time in Georgia. Georgia and Texas for Ranger School. That's the closest I've been to the Deep South."

"You're not from Connecticut though?"

"Sure I am. Why not? I'm not from Chester, that's true enough. I grew up in Smithfield. There's the Best Western sign."

I turned off the main highway and parked in the mostly empty front lot of the hotel. We got out and went around to get our bags. The air was sweet and damp, moonlight gilded the angles of the nondescript building. A light shone welcomingly in the front lobby, though the rest of the hotel was dark.

The only other sign of life was a small compact car slowly backing out of its slot, headlights sweeping the concrete drive and scraggly trees.

We had both packed light, one bag each. As we made our way across the drive, the compact rolled slowly past. The car backfired, the bang carrying through the silent night. Kirk, walking slightly ahead of me, went down like he'd been shot.

For a confused instant, I thought he'd tripped. Then I registered his position, the white knuckles, braced shoulders, wild eyes, and I understood he had dove for the ground.

I dropped my own bag, kneeling beside him. "Kirk, are you okay?"

"Fine," he said thickly, head down.

The compact braked, windows rolled down, and a couple of girls my age were inquiring if we were all right?

"Fuck off," Kirk muttered, shoving up on his hands and knees. "Just fuck off."

"Great!" I called, waving them on. "He just missed the step." And no wonder, seeing that there wasn't one.

"Are you sure?"

"Yep! We're good."

They ducked back inside the car, and the compact sped away. I tried to help Kirk up, and nearly got shoved on my ass for my trouble. He got to his feet, and raked both hands through his hair so that it stood out like his own personal storm cloud.

"Are you sure you're okay?" I shut up at the look he gave me.

He stooped and picked up his carryall, slinging it over his shoulder, and stalked away through the sliding glass doors. I followed.

Inside, a sleepy desk clerk checked us in, handed over our room keys, informed us about the not-to-be-missed continental breakfast, and directed us past the racks of travel brochures and giant potted plants to the elevator.

Inside the elevator, Kirk said nothing, staring fiercely straight ahead as though he was by himself. I didn't know what to say. That one glimpse of his dazed face — that naked terror and rage — had shocked me speechless. It was an unauthorized peek into another man's private hell, and I knew firsthand how hard it was to forgive someone for seeing that. For Kirk's sake I wished there was a way to unsee it.

"You're not going to pay for your plane fare," I said as the second floor slid past. "And I want to reimburse you for your hotel room."

Kirk shook his head.

"You're only here because of me, and I plan on deducting this trip's expense off whatever I make from selling Uncle Winston's collection; so yes, absolutely I'm reimbursing you." I met his dark, hollow gaze. "I don't know that I could do this without you."

A muscle moved in his jaw. He said stiffly, "Whatever. I'm not going to pretend I have money to burn."

We reached the third floor, our floor. The elevator doors slid open with a loud ding. Silently we walked along the narrow hall. The rooms were next to each other, which I thought was handy, though I didn't say so. Kirk slid his key card in and pushed his door open.

"What time tomorrow?"

I hesitated. "I was hoping to get an early start, but if you —"

"Just give me a time."

"Nine?"

"Nine. I'll meet you downstairs in the lobby." He stepped inside his room, then looked out again. "I'm going downstairs to work out in the Fitness Center. If you need me, that's where I'll be."

"Okay. Goodnight."

His door slid heavily into the frame and automatically locked.

CHAPTER TWELVE

Plump and grimy angels, some cracked, some missing heads or wings, some with features obliterated by moss giving them a leprous appearance, perched on short columns positioned regularly along the long sweeping drive to the main house of Bellehaven Plantation.

"Nice," Kirk commented, gazing out the rental car window. "Maybe we're on the right track after all."

West Feliciana Parish's great claim to fame was having more plantations open for public tours than anywhere else in Louisiana — and possibly the entire South. All eight plantation homes were within a twelve mile radius of St. Francisville, but the word was that any of the other seven would be preferable to visit than Bellehaven. In fact, Polly, the Southern Belle in Training at the Best Western front desk, told us not to waste our time on Bellehaven, concluding, "I don't know how them folks stay in business."

"But it *is* open weekdays this time of year?"

"I guess so. I don't know many folks who bother to go out there. At Oakley House you can visit with Gus, the talking turkey."

"Hmm," Kirk said. "That's pretty tempting. What do you think, Flynn?"

"Could you tell us how to get to Bellehaven?"

Kirk and Polly exchanged commiserating looks.

"Can you imagine what Gus would have to say about this?" I said now. "Even the trees look depressed. What do they call those droopy ones? Are those weeping willows?"

Kirk made an amused sound. "That's Spanish moss growing on live oak. You see a lot of it on cypress and oak around here."

I was happy to note Kirk was back to his normal dour self this morning. He'd made a serious dent in the continental breakfast supplies for the next month, grazing his way through fruit and cereal and yogurt, so his appetite was healthy enough and he seemed alert and ready for action.

Not that I pictured much demand for Ranger type skills in the next few hours. Now that we were here, I was wondering at the impulse that had driven me to drop everything and fly down to Louisiana. The odds of actually finding out anything useful were pretty slim. Plus I didn't even like gumbo.

"What do you think those old shacks are?" I asked, braking to let what appeared to be an armadillo waddle across the road and vanish into the undergrowth of camellia bushes.

"Slave cabins? It's the Deep South, Flynn. Who do you think worked these plantations?"

"I know who worked the plantations. I just thought maybe those were smokehouses."

"Smokehouses? Are you sure you didn't think they were guest cottages?"

"What the hell, Kirk?" I said, starting to get genuinely irritated.

"You're from Virginia. You grew up in the Shenandoah Valley. Don't try to tell me you never saw any traces of the Confederacy or slavery before."

"Am I arguing with you?" I added shortly, "All I can tell you is Louisiana is a lot different from Virginia. Even the Shenandoah Valley."

"I'll take your word for it."

"Damn Yankee," I added darkly.

Kirk's laugh was friendlier.

We reached the end of the drive and parked beside a Volkswagen van that looked like it had been there since the 1960s. Mounds of pink and red azaleas formed a tall hedge, and beyond the hedge was Bellehaven House. Neither of us said anything as we gazed out the windshield. Beneath stormy skies, the plantation house stood on a slight hill overlooking the remaining 150 acres of the estate. Two stories tall, not counting the belvedere, surrounded by a stately colonnade and second floor gallery with lacy iron railings, Bellehaven was the classic antebellum mansion. From a distance it looked untouched by time. I could easily imagine women in enormous hoop skirts and gentlemen in uniform promenading along the wide covered porch.

To the east of the house was a large pond surrounded by flowering shrubs and trees. On the west side sat a small gazebo with what appeared to be stained glass panels.

"Wow," I said finally. "It looks like it should be starring in a very special episode of *Ghost Hunters*."

"No shit." Even Kirk sounded impressed. "Your ghost left a prime piece of real estate behind when she lit out for Connecticut."

"Maybe she got tired of mint juleps."

"Or jambalaya."

I took a deep breath. "Okay. If I start speaking French hit me with the nearest spinning wheel."

"Roger that."

We got out of the car. The mild air was threaded with the fragrance of wild honeysuckle, decayed wood and the promise of rain, though it was not raining yet. We made our way through a rickety arbor, past a sign reading:

HOME OF JOHN JAMES WHITAKER, NOTORIOUS RIVERBOAT PIRATE BEFORE HIS PARDON BY THE GOVERNOR OF LOUISIANA. BELLEHAVEN PLANTATION WAS BUILT IN 1780 TO GROW SUGAR CANE.

"Arrrr, pirates," I commented.

"Aye, matie," Kirk growled.

We continued up the long, pastel-hued stone walkway. Overhead, ink-edged clouds coiled and uncoiled in sinister helixes, squeezing out a few drops of smoky rain. The walk was in good shape, but the pond was choked with lilies, and the lawns were as patchy as a threadbare carpet, the flowerbeds mostly neglected. As we drew closer to the house it was plain the building had not been painted in recent memory. A couple of upstairs windows were shuttered, but others had simply been boarded up.

We went up the wide, low steps, crossed the long entry porch and went through the open doors of the once grand entrance into a reception lobby.

Despite the gloomy weather, it took my eyes a second to adjust to the even gloomier interior. The hall was huge and mostly empty. A couple of somber oil portraits decorated — to use the term loosely — the walls. Next to a roped-off grand staircase was a tall desk. On a stool behind the desk sat a trim, middle-aged woman with very short dark hair. She was absently dunking shortbread in a thermos coffee cup while she read an issue of *National Geographic*.

She jumped at the sound of our footsteps and nearly fell off her stool.

"Good morning," I called across the empty expanse of wooden floor. "We're here for the tour."

"Good morning!" Her voice echoed back. "Welcome to Bellehaven House. I'm afraid the tour is pretty much self-serve. But I'll be happy to answer any questions you have. My name's Daphne."

"How much is the self-serve tour, Daphne?" Kirk asked as we reached the desk.

"Er...five dollars, but it all goes to the maintenance and upkeep of the house and grounds."

Kirk's look was what they call *speaking*.

"Sure," I said. "I'm all for historical preservation." I dug my wallet out and paid the fees.

Daphne was looking more cheerful by the moment. But her face fell when I asked, "Is the house haunted?"

"Not really. If you really want haunts, you should try The Myrtles. They've got all kinds of ghosties and bogles over there."

"That's okay. This is the house we're interested in," I assured her. "Can we start looking around? Is there any area off limits?"

"The upstairs is closed off while we do renovations."

That was disappointing, especially as I couldn't see any sign of renovations in progress.

"You said 'not really,'" Kirk observed. "Does that mean you *have* seen some things around here?"

Daphne laughed self-consciously. "Well, we're usually here by ourselves all day long in this giant old barn of a place. It's only natural that our imaginations are going to get the better of us now and again."

"See, that sounds promising," I said. "Are there any stories to go with the ghosts?"

"Now! I didn't say there were ghosts."

"Yeah, but you hinted."

She chuckled. "Well, it's true sometimes we all get the feeling we're being watched. And of course, we are." She nodded at a security camera in the corner. "Truth to tell, sometimes I think I see someone out of the corner of my eye or I'll get the impression that someone is standing just behind me. Of course there's never anything there."

I surprised myself with a shiver, and Kirk laughed like he thought I was kidding, but Daphne's experience was unsettlingly familiar. "Is the house still owned by the original family?"

"No, no. The Whitakers died out in the forties. The house went to some distant cousins New Orleans way. They sold most everything in the fifties, auctioned it all off except for the few pieces you'll see here in the house today."

"So who owns the place now?" Kirk tipped his head back to study the ornate ceiling medallions.

"The family name is Bankston. I think they leave it all to the property management company. That's who we deal with."

"My uncle bought a mirror here in the fifties. It's a beautiful piece. I guess that would have been when most of the furnishings were auctioned off."

Daphne nodded. "That sounds about right. Everything of real value that wasn't nailed down was sold. That's what I've heard."

"Is there anyone still around from that time?"

She looked interested. "What time would that be?"

"The fifties, I guess." I looked self-consciously at Kirk. He raised his brows, offering no help.

"I'm sure there are. I was born in the fifties. Lots of folks were!"

"Why don't we take a look around?" Kirk suggested.

"You be sure to come back with any questions," Daphne said, returning to her magazine and coffee.

It didn't take us long to explore the downstairs of the twenty room mansion. The floor plan was simple and the bones of the house were still beautiful. Hardwood floors and floor to ceiling windows that could be raised into a recess so as to remove the wall between the terrace and parlors. A fifteen foot wide central hall ran from the front to the rear on both floors. Among the rooms on the first floor were the kitchen, double parlor, library, dining room, and powder room.

"It's a shame this has all gone to hell," Kirk commented as the floorboards creaked beneath our footsteps.

"It would cost a fortune to renovate this and another fortune to maintain it. Do you think a ghost can be in two places at once?"

"Huh?" Kirk turned away from his examination of a bookcase stuffed with leather volumes. Nothing of real value; I'd already checked. Once an antique dealer, always an antique dealer.

"If Daphne and the gang are experiencing paranormal activity here, it can't be related to our lady in black, can it?"

"You're asking the wrong person."

"Or maybe it can."

"Maybe there's something in the water here."

We walked into the dining room. It was obviously the dining room because there was a dining table and chairs, but the table was dwarfed by the enormous space. It looked like a set of playhouse furniture on a bathmat. Maybe not quite that bad, but originally the room would have been a showpiece, furnished with imported art and textiles as well as fine European furniture. The museum staff had done its best to fill in with the pieces available, but it was obvious that with the exception of the faded wallpaper, and a French cut glass and ormolu chandelier, nothing in the room was original to it.

At the far end, a large round mirror in a gold leaf frame hung over a fireplace. I walked over to the mirror. Kirk appeared behind me, his reflection tall and dark and a little piratical compared to my own blond, spiky haired image. He was a good head taller than me and a lot broader.

He scowled at his reflection and said, "I'm glad I don't shave. I'm kind of leery of looking in mirrors these days."

"I thought it was just me. I'm thinking of growing a beard."

"Nah. It wouldn't suit you."

"I'm tired of getting carded every time I order a beer or a glass of wine."

"You'd just look like a little kid with a fake beard."

"How do you know what I'd look like with a beard?"

He shrugged.

I said, "Well, you look like one of those portraits in the main hall. Only not so cheerful."

He laughed.

I peered more closely at the discolored wallpaper. "Does the wallpaper around the mirror look darker to you?" I stepped back, narrowly avoiding his feet, and stared up at the wall. "Hey, look at this."

He joined me and we both silently inspected the wall. Once you knew what to look for, the subtly darker cartouche outline stuck out like a giant thumb print.

"This is where the mirror hung," I said. "After it was sold, they didn't have anything large enough to cover this much wall space."

"The dining room?" Kirk said skeptically.

"Why not?"

Kirk shook his head. "I don't know. I just never thought of that mirror hanging in a dining room."

"Where did you think it would hang?"

"Bedroom."

"Kinky."

His cheeks got that pink tinge again. I grinned at him. I liked Kirk a lot right then.

He said brusquely, "So why would the lady in black be haunting the dining room? She didn't like the food?"

"I don't know, but this is definitely where that mirror hung."

We moved on to the library, pausing to study the displays of photos, neatly labeled with brief biographical details. The first series were Civil War era. Young men in Confederate uniform, women in hoops and high collars, solemn-eyed children who had died young. Granted, when the size of the average litter was seven, someone usually survived to carry on the line. There were photographs of the house and of slaves.

In the next series of photos there were shots of the gardens, early automobiles, self-conscious young couples, and more children who had died early. There was a pair of brothers in World War I uniform. One of the brothers never turned up in another photo. The other brother married.

"Kirk," I said urgently. "Look at this." He joined me in front of the yellowed wedding portrait. "Is that her?"

"Is it?"

I peered more closely. "I think so. Maybe."

"I don't recognize her without the mist and glowing eyes."

I bit my lip. "Maybe a younger version? A happier version?"

Kirk shook his head. "Maybe. She looks..."

"Spanish?"

"French?"

"Not like anybody else in this family, that's for sure." The Whitakers were uniformly of the Anglo-Saxon variety.

I looked below the photo for the type-written caption. "*Edward Whitaker marries Ines Villars, 1928.* So she's French."

"Probably French Creole," Kirk said. "Given that we're a stone's throw from New Orleans." His eyes met mine. "In 1928 that must have been complicated."

I wasn't up on my Louisiana history, let alone Creole history, so I had no comment. I studied the subsequent photos. There were two of Ines. One looked like some kind of ladies society gathering. A lot of prune faces and knees pressed tight together. Not Ines though. Her profile was half-turned from the camera and she looked ready to get up and walk away. I couldn't blame her.

"The local coven," Kirk said, looking over my shoulder.

"Ha." I liked his aftershave. I'd never noticed it before.

The other photo was of Edward and Ines in historical costume, as though heading out for a fancy dress ball.

"Kirk, what do you think of this one?" He leaned in again. "That black lace mantilla. That's what I saw that night."

I didn't have to explain which night. We were neither of us likely to forget.

"Are you sure? Those fancy dress costumes all look pretty much the same. Even back then."

"It's her. I know it."

He grunted.

I moved along the photo display but there were no more photos of Edward or Ines.

"What do you think happened to her?" I asked.

"That's what we're here to find out, I guess." Kirk added, "It's not like this is a complete photographic record. In fact, it's pretty hit or miss."

I nodded.

"Do you know anything about Ines Villars?" I asked Daphne when we returned to the rotunda and the reception desk.

Daphne made a regretful face. "Not really. Neither Ines or Edward are what you'd call our stars."

"They aren't?"

"Not really no. There just isn't enough information to really play them up. Now the Captain, he's one of our stars. He's our biggest star. And his daughter Belle, she's another one. *She* was a wild one. Talk about emancipated! She even wrote her memoirs. Pretty hot stuff for those days, I hear. And Colonel Jeffery Whitaker. He's very popular. So sad. He died just a few days after Lee surrendered."

"You don't know anything about Ines Villars?"

Just that both she and Edward died in 1933. There was an outbreak of influenza. Edward's cousin Thomas Whitaker inherited Bellehaven."

"Influenza?" Definitely not what I had been expecting.

"It was a very serious illness in those days."

"I know. I was just expecting something more..." Dramatic. Something that would result in a spirit unable to lie quiet in her grave. My phone rang. I hastily fished it out and swore inwardly. "Excuse me," I said to Daphne.

"There are chairs and tables out on the veranda. Not that anyone ever uses them." She smiled. "Just follow the hallway all the way to the end."

I nodded, already walking.

"Hi, Mom," I said, as I stepped out onto the wide veranda. Dead leaves from the previous fall crunched underfoot. "What's up?" I really did love my mom, but could her timing have been worse?

My briskness flustered her, but Mom had cracked tougher nuts than me, and she regrouped fast. "Flynn, honey. I just wanted to say hello and hear how things are going."

This was the moment to fess up and let the parental units know where I was and what I was up to — or at least offer the abridged version, minus the French-speaking ghostly possession parts. I considered the truth, and instinctively rejected it.

"Mom, there's a Royal Vienna cabinet plate signed by Knoellez. I think Uncle Winston was using it for his supper."

"Oh my."

"There's a set of cordial glasses here that might be vintage Saint Louis."

"That's exciting. Flynn, Dr. Kirsch phoned and said you haven't been in contact with him since you left for Connecticut."

I didn't have to fake my surprise. "Dr. Kirsch? Dr. Kirsch isn't part of the agreement."

"Honey." I could hear how careful she was being. "Dr. Kirsch is your psychiatrist. Part of the agreement — the *other* agreement — was that he would continue to oversee your treatment. You're supposed to check in with him once a week. Dr. Kirsch said he hasn't heard from any of the local doctors on the referral list either."

I sat down on the little wrought iron bench. I couldn't seem to think of anything to say.

My mother asked in that unhappy, tentative tone so unlike her usual one, "Flynn, honey, have you contacted any of those therapists yet? Have you made an appointment to see someone?"

"No."

"Oh, *honey.*"

I tried to think of something to say.

"Flynn." The too-quiet note in her voice dried my mouth. "Dr. Kirsch has been checking your pharmacy records and he says you haven't refilled any of your prescriptions. You promised me that you were taking your medications."

"I didn't promise." I stopped.

"Flynn, the medication isn't optional. You *have* to take it. You know that."

My heart began to thump against my ribs. "I don't — didn't realize…" I heard how breathy and unsteady I sounded and closed my mouth. I closed my eyes too.

My mother said nothing.

Fuck. Fuck. Fuck. Oh fuck you, Kirsch. Dirty pool, you arrogant, busybody asshole. You don't know everything. You don't know me.

Still nothing from my mother. What happened now? Were they going to flip out and insist I come home? Or worse, much worse, head for Connecticut — and then discover I wasn't there, which would undoubtedly precipitate widespread panic and revoking of parole?

My mother's too-long silence was suddenly broken by my father's crisp voice.

"Flynn?"

I squinched my face so tight I was afraid I'd pop my cheekbones. I managed a gruff, "Sir?"

He asked gently, "Okay, son?"

For one really horrifying moment I feared I was going to break down. "Yeah," I got out. "I guess I didn't…" I forced myself onward. "…understand that I was still…" I saw motion out of the corner of my eye. Kirk was walking toward me. I jumped up and started in the opposite direction.

I didn't want Kirk to hear this. *I* didn't want to hear it. I wanted to believe that was all behind me now. It felt like it was behind me. Maybe that was the payoff for all the spooky craziness. It forced the other craziness into the background.

"Of course you're not," my father said with absolute and reassuring certainty. "But even if this is just a formality, there's a process in place, and it's going to cause less wear and tear on everybody's nerves if we stick to the plan."

"Yes." I swallowed hard. "Agreed."

"You have to take the meds."

"Dad, I feel better without them. Really. I don't think they're right for me."

"Then that's something to talk over with Dr. Kirsch when you see him next month. Until then, you need to take your medication. Understood?"

I said humbly, "Yes, sir."

He said in an easy, perfectly ordinary tone, "Other than forgetting to make those appointments, how are things going up there?"

And just like that everything was back in perspective. I wasn't going to be locked up or dragged home. I wasn't getting busted down to private. I was still an autonomous adult.

"It's a hell of a lot of work, which is what I want. And need."

"Good. I'm glad to hear it. Just remember to stop and eat once in a while."

He was teasing and I didn't have to force a smile into my voice, my relief genuine. "I will. I am."

"I love you, son. Your mother too."

That was Dr. Kirsch's influence. I had grown up never doubting for a second that I was loved, but now every phone call ended with declarations. Even from my dad. But…I didn't really mind.

"I know. Love you, Dad," I said. "Love to Mom. I'll talk to you in a couple of days." It took me two tries to disconnect; my hands were still shaky. I started back to meet Kirk.

"What's up?" he asked.

"Nothing. My parents checking in. They know I don't like it when they stay out past their curfew."

He studied my face. "Right. So is that it? Have you seen enough here?"

I looked back at the silent, shuttered house. "I don't know. It feels like it's a dead end."

"Yeah. That's because it is a dead end. All we really learned here is Ines died a long time ago, and we already knew that."

"Now we know *how* she died."

"And that helps us how?"

I shook my head. "The more we know, the more chance of figuring out what she wants, right?"

"It depends on the quality of information. So far, I don't think we've found anything particularly earthshaking."

"Well, something's keeping her up at night."

"True. But I don't think we're going to find an answer here. I think this trip is a waste of time and money. But it's your time and your money."

I laughed without humor. "See, that's what I like about you, Kirk. You don't pull your punches."

He asked seriously, "Do you want me to pull my punches?"

I didn't have to think about it. "No. I don't."

He gave me a grim smile. "And that's what I like about *you*, Flynn."

CHAPTER THIRTEEN

"There has to be some kind of historical society around here," I said as we started back down the hillside. A pair of crows, blue-black wings shining in the fitful light, skimmed overhead, laughing raucously. "This entire parish has made a going concern out of the past. *And* we can still see about getting the video translated."

"I guess."

"I admit I figured the way she died would probably explain everything. That's how it works in the ghost stories. Someone dies a terrible, violent death. Or they've left some quest unfulfilled. Or the person doesn't realize they're dead."

"I think she knows she's dead."

That was an interesting idea. *Did* Ines know she was dead? "So then maybe it's one of the other reasons. Maybe she left some quest unfulfilled?"

Kirk made an exasperated sound.

I said, "A ghost has to have a reason to hang around."

"Says who?"

"Think about how angry she — it — seemed. It was ranting. Raving."

"The flu makes everyone cranky."

"I'm serious."

"There must be a college or a junior college nearby," Kirk said finally. "We'll contact their language arts department. I'm sure we can find someone to help us out."

"But we have to be careful about who we show that video to," I couldn't help adding.

Kirk slanted a look my way. "I wasn't planning to schedule it for the fall season lineup."

"I know. I'm paranoid."

"Yeah?"

"Actually, no." I nerved myself. "But since we're on the subject, can I ask you exactly what my parents told you about me?"

Kirk's gaze was direct, his tone easy. "Sure. You're suffering from depression and they're concerned. However, they both assured me they trusted you to keep to the terms of your agreement. You are a man of your word."

"Did they tell you what the agreement was?" I asked warily.

"No. I think the real reason your mother phoned was because she believed that I was naturally smitten with your boyish charms and she wanted to warn me not to try to jump your bones, however irresistible. I got the impression that if I so much as bruised your feelings she'd cut off my balls and serve them to me for breakfast with my hash browns."

Horror kept me silent. Somehow I kept walking, putting one foot in front of the other.

"She put it more elegantly, of course," Kirk said. "But I read her loud and clear."

"I-I don't know what to say."

Kirk made a noise of acrid amusement. "Your father's concern is that the house is a death trap and you might try to fix the wiring yourself. Apparently your handyman skills are limited."

"Once," I said indignantly. "*Once* I crossed a couple of wires with the garage door opener. You'd think I blew up the neighborhood!"

"Okay, Thomas Edison. Don't shoot the messenger."

"For the record, I replaced the garbage disposal unit at my old place." With Alan's help. Funny how long ago that seemed.

"I think the memory of that turns him faint with horror. Anyway, his other worry was that there was no suitable kitchen. Apparently you're an excellent cook when you want to be, which makes me think we might be able to work out some kind of trading goods for services. My handyman skills are up to the minute."

"Maybe," I said grudgingly. I still felt hot and uncomfortable at these revelations. It probably would have been better not knowing. "I love my parents, but sometimes..."

Kirk chuckled. "They seem like nice people. You're clearly their fair haired boy. My old man took off when I was nine. I never saw him again. As for my mother, I don't think a single day went by we didn't fight when I was growing up. I couldn't get away from home fast enough. I joined the army when I turned eighteen and I haven't been back since."

I didn't know what to say to that. Underneath his brusque exterior, Kirk was one of the kindest people I'd ever known. How did someone like that come from a background like his? My mom talked a lot about nature versus nurture, but it seemed to me Kirk had both against him.

A high pitched voice was yelling behind us. Kirk stopped in his tracks. I turned. Daphne trotted down the uneven walk, calling to us.

She reached us, flushed and out of breath, and handed over a scrap of paper. "Maryann Kleinpeter. She mans the front desk here the days I don't. Her mother, Violet, used to work for the Whitakers."

"Is she still alive?"

Daphne looked briefly exasperated, "Yes, she's still alive. You do seem determined to put all of us over thirty in our graves!"

Kirk laughed. I ignored him. "Is she willing to talk to us, do you think?"

"Willing to talk your ear off, if I know Violet. You give Maryann a call. You'll hear some stories, I guarantee you."

* * * * *

"That was a sad day," Violet Gallot said, smiling faintly as Maryann topped off our glasses of sweet tea. "The saddest day in the history of Bellehaven House. Everything of real value went on the auction block, including old John James Whitaker's bed. To this moment I remember that bed. It was enormous and kinda shaped like a ship's galleon."

Kirk choked on his tea, though that might have been the sugary sweetness of it. It was certainly the sweetest tea I'd ever drunk. It was served with warm corn bread which was fantastic.

Maryann and her mother lived in a little white house on a shady street in St. Francisville. Coral and pink azaleas lined the porch. A faded sign planted in the tidy, green lawn urged reelection for Mayor Billy D'Aquilla. The wreath on the front door was twined with red, white, and blue ribbons. The inside of the house matched the outside for neat-and-orderliness. The furniture had been repainted many times, and there was an abundance of craft project décor: wall stencils and cornice boards and slip covers.

Violet continued, "But there were just two elderly maiden aunts left in New Orleans, and what were they going to do with that great old house and all its furnishings?"

Maryann said, "It's a sad story, but it's a common one in these parts." She was about Daphne's age, blonde and plump and cheerful. Her mother was probably in her early eighties, smaller, thinner, darker. Her white hair was bobby-pinned; a purple flowered scarf tied turban style around her head. Also, she was blind, but we'd been talking a little while before I realized it, Violet was so good at functioning without sight.

"How long did you work at Bellehaven, ma'am?" Kirk asked.

"From the time I was a little bit of a thing," Violet said. "I started as a chamber maid when I was sixteen. I moved up to parlor maid, then head house maid. Of course by then there were only three of us left."

I said, "So in 1933..."

"Violet would have been a gleam in her daddy's eye," Kirk said.

Violet laughed. "Not quite, but close enough. My Auntie Corinne was housekeeper at Bellehaven for forty years. She got me my position there when I left school. So I still might be able to help you with your questions."

"Do you remember the mirror my uncle purchased that day at auction? Very large with a heavy gold frame carved with flowers and fruit and a basket."

Was there a lull in the conversation? I wasn't sure. It felt like the space between the struggle for breaths. A suffocated kind of pause.

Violet laughed uneasily, "There were a lot of mirrors sold that day."

"This might have been originally purchased by John James himself. It would have been quite old and very valuable, even back then."

Violet was shaking her head. "There was a lot of very valuable things sold that day. All the toys in the nursery. All the dolls and the tin soldiers and the clockwork animals. There was a gray dappled rocking horse with a white mane and tail made of real pony hair."

As I listened to Violet I thought two things. First, that she was lying about not remembering the mirror. I couldn't imagine why she'd bother since I already knew the mirror had come from Bellehaven. There wasn't any concealing that. The second thing that struck me was her talking about the nursery and the toys. The memory of the mirror had prompted her to think of the nursery. What connected those two things in her mind?

"More cornbread?" Maryann asked.

"No thank you," I said. "It was great though."

"Yes, ma'am. Please." Kirk held his plate out.

"Someone needs to fatten you up, child," Maryann said to me. She beamed approvingly at Kirk.

We drank our tea and ate cornbread. The rain ticked in absent and erratic fashion against the windows.

"Is Bellehaven haunted?" I asked.

Maryann laughed, but her mother looked thoughtful. "They say you can see old John James's sloop sailing up the Mississippi on moonlight summer nights."

"What about the house itself?"

Violet shook her head. "I never saw anything. You'll want to visit The Myrtles if it's ghosts you're hunting, child."

"I've never seen or heard anything," Maryann said staunchly.

I wondered what she'd heard. I looked at Kirk.

He said, "John James's line died out with Edward, is that right?"

Violet nodded somberly. Again I had the impression that she was waiting, listening for something.

"Correct," Maryann said. She folded her hands and looked expectant, awaiting the next question.

"And that was during the influenza epidemic of 1933?"

"Correct," Maryann said again.

Violet said nothing. She didn't move a muscle. I'd rarely heard such a loud silence.

"And Edward's wife was also carried off in the influenza epidemic?" Kirk asked.

"Correct," Maryann replied, making it three for three.

Violet reached for her tea, lifted the glass without spilling a drop, and sipped noiselessly.

Kirk looked at me.

I said, "I guess that's it then. Thank you for all your help. We should really get going now."

Violet seemed to still with surprise.

"While I'm thinking of it," I began. "Is there a college nearby? A junior college? I wanted to get some French translated."

"Oh lordy," Maryann exclaimed. "You don't need to go to college for that. Amy Madison teaches French at West Feliciana high school. Amy'd be happy to help. She's a sweet little thing. She's teaching school right now, but she gets home around two-thirty."

"Amy has choir practice this evening," Violet said.

Maryann said, "Mama, you're right. Well, if you boys would like to leave your book or whatever it is. Or you could just come back after lunch?"

"It's kind of complicated," I said. "It's actually a video on my phone. It might even be French Creole being spoken."

"I see," Maryann said, looking more puzzled than ever. "Then why don't you boys come back later and we'll see if Amy can't help you out."

"That's very nice of you, ma'am," Kirk said. "But we don't want to put you to any more trouble. Do you have Amy's phone number?"

Maryann looked disappointed. "Of course!" She rose.

Violet said quietly, "Why do you want to know?"

"I'm sorry?" I looked at Violet.

Violet's sightless gaze turned my direction. "Why are you asking these questions? What is it you're trying to find out?"

Kirk's dark eyes warned me to proceed with caution, but it seemed to me that Violet wouldn't have asked if she wasn't considering breaking her silence. "I want to know what really happened to Edward and Ines."

"Why?"

"I need to know the truth."

"Why, child? Why would you need to know the truth about something that ended long before you were born?"

I had to consider a couple of different answers. Over the past few months I'd got so in the habit of concealing the truth from those likely to use it against me that lying had become instinct. The truth did not always set you free. Sometimes it got you locked up. Sometimes for your own protection. Sometimes it got you killed.

So it was with surprise and relief that I heard Kirk's calm, "Because sometimes you can't move forward until you understand the past."

Simple and absolute truth.

Violet nodded to herself. Her daughter looked curiously from her to us.

Finally, Violet said, "Let's hear what little Amy has to say about this mysterious translation of yours. I can't make promises, but maybe it *is* time for the dead to tell their story."

* * * * *

Judging by the number of trucks and cars in the parking lot, the locals seemed to like the Audubon Café for lunch, so Kirk and I headed over there for burgers.

"I've got news for Violet," I said, as the waitress departed after delivering our meals. "The dead are already telling their story. What I can't understand is why, after all this time, anyone would lie about people who've been dead nearly a century." I watched Kirk tuck into a sourdough melt with browned onions. How he could stuff anything else down his throat after half a plate of corn bread was a mystery. "I think Daphne and Maryann wouldn't notice a ghost if it threw a sheet over their heads. But Violet is definitely not telling everything she knows."

"That's not the same as lying. Some people call that discretion. It used to be highly prized in a servant. And a neighbor. And a friend. And maybe Aunt Corinne was all those things to the Whitakers. Maybe Violet inherited that attitude."

"Did people like the Whitakers think of people like Aunt Corinne as anything but servants?"

"I don't know. John James was a river pirate. The Whitakers lost most of their fortune in the Civil War. Maybe deep down they were humble folk."

I shook my head. "They didn't look like humble folks in the photographs. What do you think did happen to Edward and Ines? I'm starting to think they didn't die of influenza. Or if they did, there was more to it than that."

"Yeah, I think there was more to it than that," Kirk agreed. He nodded at my plate. "Can I give you some advice?"

"Don't eat the pickles?"

"Eat your lunch. And your dinner. And your breakfast. Eat right. Sleep right. Exercise a lot. That's half the battle."

"My shrink will be thrilled to hear it."

Kirk was unsmiling, dead serious. He took another giant-sized bite of his burger.

I said, "There's something about the mirror too. Violet did recognize it from my description. I'm pretty sure."

Kirk chewed thoughtfully. "There must be a family graveyard. It's probably still part of the Bellehaven Estate. If not, there will be a parish churchyard, church records, that kind of thing."

"That's a *great* idea."

He smiled faintly. "Of course it's possible the graves corroborate the official version of Edward and Ines's deaths. It's likely no one but the immediate family and servants ever knew the whole truth. Assuming there is a 'whole' truth. We're making a lot of assumptions based on our amateur interpretation of a couple of paranormal events."

"But doesn't a paranormal event in itself indicate…well, something?"

"Flynn, we don't even know what a ghost *is*. Maybe it's a trapped soul looking for vindication. Or justice. Or the back exit. We're just guessing. Is it a psychic echo? A spiritual imprint that operates like a broken record, replaying a certain event over and over. Is it a collective hallucination?"

"Don't stop there," I said. "Maybe I'm schizophrenic. Maybe *I'm* Ines. *Voilà!*"

Kirk, about to wrap his mouth around another bite of sandwich, froze, eyes fixed on me. He started to laugh. He laid the remaining scrap of sandwich on his plate.

"Glad you find it so funny."

"Look, I'm not denying that we are dealing with…" he glanced around and lowered his voice "…some kind of supernatural phenomenon. We're both on the same page as far as that goes. I've seen what you've seen — and then some. But where we go from here, I don't know. Neither of us does."

"Because we haven't heard the whole story. We don't know what Ines wants."

"We don't know that our ghost *is* Ines. We could be looking at the wrong decade. At the wrong century."

"I *know* the woman in black is Ines."

He considered me. "Say it *is* Ines. Say we learn that Ines didn't die of influenza, she ran off with the chauffeur or Colonel Beauregard, and everybody hushed it up. How are you going to fix that? How are you going to set it right for Ines? Why would Ines need it set right? Wouldn't it be Edward who needed things put right?"

"Maybe Edward ran off with the chauffeur." But I'd been thinking that point over myself, and I didn't really have an answer. Still, I said stubbornly, "According to the legends I've read — and a couple of episodes of *Paranormal State* — just having the truth revealed, usually sets the spirit free."

"See, I think our spirit is too free already. I want to know how to get her back in her grave. For good."

I pushed back my chair. "Okay. Let's do it. Let's start there. Let's go find where Ines and Edward are buried."

Kirk studied me for a moment. He pushed his chair back.

*   *   *   *   *

"Back so soon?" Daphne greeted us in surprise. "We're having record crowds today." She nodded toward an elderly couple quietly discussing the morose family portraits lining the central hall.

"We missed the graveyard when we were here earlier," I said.

"You're determined to get your money's worth, aren't you." She was amused. "You passed the family cemetery on the drive up to the house." She picked up one of the colorful and highly misleading brochures, and opened it to a map of the grounds. "There we are. It's right there." She glanced up from the map. "You can see the top of the marble tomb belonging to John James from the road. There's a mermaid holding a shell."

"A mermaid?"

"I suppose she's kind of a mermaid angel." Daphne looked thoughtful. "He was a pirate, after all."

We thanked her, turned around, and returned down the hill. The rain was a soft, white mist around us, swallowing our footsteps. The air smelled of wet earth and warm flowers. Every so often something rustled in the undergrowth, but whatever was wandering around the old plantation, whether wild hog or armadillo, was too shy to make an appearance.

"You should be happy," I said to Kirk. "We're getting our exercise for the day."

"Can't you tell how happy I am?"

Once we reached the main road it didn't take long to locate the cemetery. Sure enough there was a mermaid quietly and eternally preening, face to the sun, on the tomb of John James Whitaker. No fence stood around the cemetery and we could walk freely among the tumbled statues and half sunken gravestones. It didn't take us long to locate the graves we were hunting.

In Memory of
Edward James Hammond Whitaker
July 3rd 1887 - February 15th 1933
Died of Influenza

"Here we go," Kirk said.

Ines Whitaker
Wife of Edward
April 11th 1911 - February 15th 1933

"Short and sweet."

"No kidding."

I said, "It doesn't state she died of the influenza. But then they weren't wasting words, were they?"

"No. But they died on the same day."

"I didn't realize how much older Edward was. You can't really tell from the photo." My gaze fell on the plain gravestone next to Ines's. "Kirk, look at this."

He moved next to me.

"There was a child," I said at last.

"Yes."

We stared down in silence.

Charles Edward Whitaker
Beloved son of Edward and Ines
February 10th 1933
Oh for the touch of a vanished hand
And the sound of a voice that is still.

CHAPTER FOURTEEN

Amy Madison was a tall, slender, sloe-eyed twenty-something. She looked like an African American Audrey Hepburn. She even spoke in that soft, deliberate Audrey style. At least until we showed her the video clip of me doing my Talking Dead routine.

"What the heck is that supposed to be?" she demanded, staring from me to Kirk then back to me again.

We were once more in Maryann and Violet's parlor. That had been Amy's suggestion, and I couldn't blame her for not wanting to meet two strange men alone in her own home. Judging by her current expression, she clearly felt she'd made the right move.

"Do you understand any of it?" I asked.

"Enough to know I don't want to understand the rest!"

"Is it French?" Kirk inquired.

"It's some archaic variant of Creole." Amy looked at him in disbelief. "What is going *on* in that video?"

"Sometimes I talk in my sleep," I said apologetically. "I never remember what I've said."

"If that's true, you need help, that's all I can say. And not my kind of help."

"So you do understand at least some of it?" Kirk pressed.

Amy glared at him. "Some. It's mostly swearing, as far as I can make out." To me, she said, "You're accusing someone," she looked at Kirk with strong dislike, "*him*, I guess, of betraying you. Of being a coward, a pig, a rapist, a murderer."

I'm pretty sure Kirk couldn't have looked more aghast than me, but it must have been a tight race. Maryann and Violet appeared pretty upset too.

I said quickly, "Not him. It's nothing to do with him. He's just a friend."

"You know some nice people!"

"I'm so sorry," I said. "I had no idea what was on that clip."

"Riiiight." Amy began gathering her things. "I'm sorry for your troubles. You've clearly got more than your share of them. But I can't listen to any more of that. I suggest you get professional counseling." She directed another look of utter loathing at Kirk.

Kirk looked so guilty that in another time and place it would have been funny.

"I will," I said. "I will definitely get help. Thank you for your time. I'm sorry about all the swear words."

"Goodnight, Maryann. Night Miz Violet." Amy gave Maryann a meaningful look.

"I'll see you to the door, Amy," Maryann responded in none-too-subtle reply. She rose.

They left the room, speaking quietly.

"I guess it's worse than I thought," I said to Kirk. Kirk nodded toward Violet. She looked tiny in a blue velveteen house coat with a flowered collar. Her hands were knotted and she was nervously licking her lips.

I moved over to the sofa and sat beside her. "Mrs. Gallot," I said. "Am I wrong in thinking maybe you know what's really going on here?"

Violet's face quivered.

"Please," I said. "I wouldn't ask, but...you can hear for yourself I need your help."

Her thin chest rose and fell. Her first words were so quiet I had to lean down to hear. "You weren't talking in your sleep. I could hear it in your voice. You were in a trance. I seen it once. At a séance in Baton Rouge when I was a girl."

"I think so, yes." I looked at Kirk. He stared down the hall and made a face, which I took to indicate Amy was giving Maryann an earful. "Strange things have been happening to me ever since I found that mirror my uncle bought from the Bellehaven Estate all those years ago." I took a deep breath. "I think I'm being haunted."

"That can't be. That can't be." Violet shook her head, but she felt for my hand and took it in her own small one. Her skin felt as dry and fragile as paper, but her grip was surprisingly strong. "Do you believe in ghosts, child?"

"I never did before. But I've seen things. Kirk's seen them too."

Violet turned her face in Kirk's direction. "Kirk is your...special friend?"

"Well, he's a friend. And he's special," I said.

Kirk rolled his eyes.

"Things are mighty different now," Violet murmured. "Back then, well." She absently patted my hand. "Your fingers are so thin. So cold. You haven't been well, child. That's why she came to you. That's why you can see her. You're standing too close to that veil between this world and the next."

I didn't bother to remind Violet that Kirk had seen "her" too, and he wasn't standing by any veil. Unless it was a beach towel. "It's Ines, isn't it?" I asked. "Ines is haunting me."

Violet nodded. "I don't see who else it could be. That mirror settles it. I remember that mirror."

"What happened? There was a baby, we know that. It was stillborn? Or it only lived a few hours. It was just a few days before Ines and Edward died."

Violet sighed. "I only know what was told to me. I wasn't there, you have to remember that."

Maryann appeared in the doorway. "My word, it's getting late. I'm afraid it's past Mama's bed —"

"Hush, Maryann," Violet said. "You sit down and don't interrupt."

"Mama!"

"Sit down and hush up!"

Maryann sat down and hushed up.

Violet squeezed my hand, as though demanding my attention. "Edward was not the oldest son. Bellehaven was supposed to go to Charles Whitaker. But Charles died during the war."

"That'll have been the Great War," Kirk said sardonically. "The War to End All Wars. Not the Late Unpleasantness."

Violet nodded. "After the war, Edward took his time settling down. He'd always been what you'd call a playboy. But finally he got to an age when he had to think about who was going to carry on the Whitaker line. He went to stay with his cousins in New Orleans, and while he was there he fell madly in love with a beautiful girl by the name of Ines Villars."

"A Creole girl," Kirk said.

"You're a smart one," Violet said approvingly. It was my turn to roll my eyes at Kirk. "But Edward didn't know that," Violet continued. "He only knew Ines was from a wealthy, well-respected old French New Orleans family."

"What would it matter?" I asked.

Kirk said, "Because after 1915 all Creoles were considered African American. If you had so much as one drop of Creole blood, you were considered African American."

"One sixteenth made you Negro," Maryann corrected automatically. "That was the law in Louisiana."

"Okay," Kirk said. "If you were even one sixteenth African American, you were considered *one hundred percent* African American and subject to racial discrimination and segregation. It didn't matter if you were a Creole of European descent or a Creole of Color, you were all lumped into the same second class citizen category."

"But weren't they the same thing? Weren't all Creoles of African descent?"

"No. Not at all. During Louisiana's colonial period Creole was just a term used to describe anyone born here who had foreign ancestors. You had French, Spanish, slaves, people of mixed race all lumped under the term 'Creole.' But after 1915 it all changed."

"And whites couldn't marry blacks."

"Yep. And it wasn't just about the legal implications of marriage. You couldn't cohabitate or have any sexual relations with a person of African heritage."

I stared at Violet. "So Ines was passing as white?"

Violet nodded. "She married Edward and came to Bellehaven to live. I guess if she had been a different sort of girl, it might have all worked out all right. But it wasn't the same way in New Orleans, and Ines was proud, strong minded, and independent. She put a lot of folks' backs up. Womenfolk, that is. She was not liked by the wives of Edward Whitaker's friends. And I don't think she tried very hard to *be* liked." Violet bit her lip. "Also there were rumors."

"There always are," Maryann put in a little bitterly.

"Nobody knows if there was any truth to the talk or not," Violet said. "Nobody ever will. I don't suppose by then it was a very happy marriage, but a marriage doesn't have to be a love affair to work well."

"Mama!"

I thought of the whole "coward, pig, rapist, murderer" matter. Yeah, probably not a match made in heaven.

Violet ignored Maryann's protest. "But then that poor little baby was born."

I guessed, "And everybody blamed Ines when the Whitaker heir died?"

Violet patted my hand comfortingly. "That was terrible of course, but the real calamity, at least from the viewpoint of Edward Whitaker, was that poor little boy was born black as coal. Black as sin."

Nobody said a word.

Violet gave a creaky giggle into that stricken silence. "You young folks are mighty easily shocked, aren't you? Well so was Edward Whitaker. He accused Ines of having an affair with a young jazz musician Baton Rouge way. But the fact is, the alternative was even worse. If Ines wasn't having an affair, if that poor little baby was just some kind of a throwback, then Edward's marriage was a sham and a disgrace and those rumors about Ines's family were true."

"Wow," I said finally. "What did Edward do?"

"He blew his brains out in the dining room. In front of Ines and the servants and that very same mirror your uncle purchased twenty years later. In fact, there was a story that no matter how many times the glass was cleaned and polished, if you looked hard enough, you could find flecks of Edward's blood and brains in the groove between the mirror and the frame."

"Eww." Maryann said weakly, "I can't believe you never told me any of this."

"It wasn't my story to tell," Violet said.

"What happened to Ines?" Kirk asked at last.

"That's not quite as clear cut. She was half crazy over losing her baby, of course, and then Edward accused her of all those terrible things, accused her of driving him to suicide right there in front of the household staff. Then Edward was gone, the validity of her marriage was in question; and there was all kinds of wild talk of putting her in prison or even worse. The only thing anyone knew for sure was her body was found later that evening floating in the little ornamental pond on the east side of the house."

Kirk said, "How the hell — heck — did a double suicide end up being attributed to influenza?"

Violet shook her head. "It was such a terrible tragedy. And, worse, such a terrible scandal, Edward's family and friends moved to hush it up. There *was* an influenza epidemic at the time, and a lot of folks were busy with their own tragedies."

"So that's it? That's the whole story?" I asked. "What happened to the jazz musician? Was Ines having an affair? Was the baby illegitimate? Did Ines drown herself?"

"That's as much as I know," Violet said wearily, shaking her head. "I believe that's as much as anyone knows. It was a very long time ago, child."

Kirk's dark gaze met mine. He said somberly, "How are you going to put *that* right, Flynn?"

* * * * *

It wasn't until we squeezed into the packed Magnolia Café for dinner that evening, and I noticed the pink and red paper hearts, streamers, and cutouts of cherubs, that I realized it was Valentine's Day.

Now I understood the urgency behind the phone call from my parents that morning. But after all, it was just another day. I stared at the items on the menu. Steaks, salads, seafood. A lot of selection. Everything from "alligator bites" to "yummy desserts." I was too tired to be hungry. It felt like the longest day of my life. Was it only last night we had flown into Baton Rouge?

Kirk ordered a NOLA Irish Channel Stout. I ordered Bayou Teche Bière Noire. The waitress asked to see my ID. I sighed, offered it, she winked and departed to fill our order.

Neither Kirk nor I had said much since we left Maryann and Violet's home. Kirk was right. I had no idea how to put the past right. The whole concept suddenly seemed ridiculous. I felt tired, even flattened every time I considered what we had learned from Violet.

I closed the menu. "The turtle soup sounds good."

"No." Kirk looked up from his own menu. His face was grim. Nothing new there. "Enough with the liquid diet. Order a real meal. Or I'll order one for you."

That took me aback. And then I got mad. "Are you going to force it down my throat too? Who died and made you my mom?"

"Do me a favor. Go take a look at yourself in the mirror in the john. You look *transparent*." His voice dropped still lower, and I realized he was genuinely angry. "You look like a goddamned ghost yourself."

"Thanks, I've had all the looking in mirrors I need for now." But I picked up the menu again. "And for your information, I *have* been eating more lately. Not that it's any of your damn business." I glanced up and Kirk was still glaring at me. "What's your problem?"

He said tightly, "My problem is you think you're going to waltz home and tackle that…thing. That thing that is waiting for you underneath the tarp in the shed of the house on Pitch Pine Lane."

I gave a disbelieving laugh. "Thanks, Kirk! I don't know why I don't have a better appetite after that."

"After everything we learned today — everything we heard this evening —"

"What's your solution?"

"You need to go home. To your real home, I mean. To your parents."

I was so angry I began to splutter — stutter, "My *real* home? My *parents*? Do you think I'm nine years old? My real home is —" *Alan*. I stopped and began again, "Pitch Pine Lane is as much my real home as anywhere else now. And yeah, I do think I'm going to have to face —" I broke off as the waitress appeared again. "Hey! What's the special tonight?" I asked brightly.

She rattled off a couple of entrees and I said, "Great! I'll have that first one." I handed her the menu and glared at Kirk.

Kirk made his selection too and handed over his menu.

The waitress withdrew and Kirk said — before I could continue my rant, "Let me deal with it. Go visit your parents for a while. Once I've got rid of the mirror, once I'm sure she — it's — gone, maybe you can come back."

I shook my head. "You're not making any sense. You can't put that mirror in cold storage on the other side of the state and think problem solved. Besides…this is mine to deal with, not yours. The mirror belongs to my family now and it's my job to…handle it."

"And you'll do that how? Tell Ines she's dead? Tell her to head for the light?"

"I don't know. Maybe." Privately I thought Ines had had long enough to figure that part out for herself.

"Or maybe you could tell her times have changed. You could explain the Civil Rights Movement to her. She might find Women's Equality interesting too."

"Shut up, Kirk." I picked up my glass and downed half my beer.

When I resurfaced Kirk was saying, "That old woman nailed it. You're too close to it. You're too close to the veil."

The veil? What the hell. Really. Honestly. The *veil*?

"You should hear yourself. Seriously. *You* should go look in the mirror."

"Did you notice the dates on the gravestones?"

"Of course! 1933. The baby died five days earlier."

"February fifteenth," Kirk bit out. "*Tomorrow*. The day we arrive home. The anniversary of Ines's death."

Okay. Fair enough. That was a shock. I didn't pay a lot of attention to time and dates now. Those things were irrelevant in a psychiatric hospital. And afterwards...I just wanted to get through the year. So no. I hadn't noticed we were on the eve of the anniversary of Edward and Ines's double suicide.

"Maybe that's a good thing," I said finally.

I thought I was about to witness spontaneous combustion, which would have given the patrons of the Magnolia Café quite a story for many a year to come, but Kirk managed to cut the blue wire in time.

He repeated, painstakingly enunciating every word, "A. Good. Thing?"

"May. Be." I was equally painstaking. "Look, I don't know. Maybe there's a pattern here. Maybe the only reason we're even seeing Ines right now is it's getting close to the anniversary. Maybe this will all be resolved February sixteenth regardless of what we do. Maybe it's a cycle."

He continued to look angry and unconvinced.

"My uncle lived with that mirror for half a century and it doesn't seem to have done him any harm."

"Flynn..."

I looked away. "Fine. I know. But I'm not going to..."

"Another round, boys?" the waitress asked cheerfully.

"Sure!" I responded. As she moved away, I said to Kirk, "Let's leave it for now. Please? I'm tired. We both are. This isn't the time to try to make a decision. So let's eat. Let's sleep. And we can argue it out tomorrow."

Kirk looked surprised. He nodded. "Fair enough."

The food was good. Good enough anyway. The conversation between Kirk and me was pretty much nonexistent, but that was okay too. I really was tired and I really didn't want to think anymore. While Kirk brooded and ate his dinner, I tried not to watch the other diners, couples all of them. Tentative new couples, affectionate older couples...not a great night for singletons to go out to dinner.

We didn't have much to say on the drive back to the hotel either.

Or in the elevator.

"What time in the morning?" Kirk asked, stopping in front of his door and pulling out his keycard.

"Eleven? That way we don't have to rush. We could have lunch on the way to the airport. I know how much your meals mean to you."

"Eleven it is." He opened his door. I moved on to mine and unlocked it.

"Night," I said.

"Night."

I turned the lights on in my room, avoided glancing at the dresser mirror, and turned on the TV. But there was nothing going on in the world I cared about.

I turned the TV off, took a shower, brushed my teeth, still avoiding looking in the foggy bathroom mirror. Was I ever not going to feel a twinge of anxiety when I looked in a mirror?

I got into bed and picked up my cell phone. No messages, no missed calls, no email. That's what happened when you shut everyone out of your life. I pressed photos and then slideshow and watched Alan's smiling face slide past.

It was almost a year now. I hadn't realized it. It still felt so new, so raw, so recent. But it had been last March. Middle of March. Eleven months. I hadn't believed I could get through the first week.

The pictures slid swiftly past. And I could remember every occasion, almost every moment. It was funny how a photograph could take you back to an exact moment in time, let you smell the fresh mown grass again, feel the sweat damping your skin, hear warm laughter against your ear, taste a mouth sweet with lemonade...

The pictures blurred and I wiped my face.

I pressed stop and laid my cell phone aside. For a few minutes I sat staring at the mustard colored drapes, listening to the invisible rain against the windows.

I shoved back the coverlet and went to the door adjoining Kirk's room with mine. I knocked softly.

Nothing.

He was probably down in the Fitness Center working off carbs. And his demons.
I turned away.

There were sounds of commotion from inside the wall and my half of the adjoining door suddenly pushed open. Kirk, wearing perfectly respectable green and blue striped pajama bottoms — and his usual frown — stood in the doorway.

"Flynn?"

"Hey."

He looked more closely, started to move, but stopped. "Are you okay?"

I tried to laugh. Had to wipe my eyes again. "This is going to sound really stupid."

"Okay." He didn't look wary, though maybe he should have. He looked calm, and I thought again how much I liked that calm of his. All the more because now I suspected how hard won it was.

I said, "I don't want a relationship. I don't even want friends with benefits. I just...don't want to be alone tonight. I don't think I can be alone tonight."

Kirk said softly, "You don't have to be alone tonight." His arms closed around me.

CHAPTER FIFTEEN

I was wrong about one thing. Kirk was a gentle man.

His arms were strong, kind, even protective as he cradled me. "What do you want?" His voice was warm and pleasantly raspy against my ear. "Do you just want me to hold you?"

"I don't know." I did know. I wanted to forget. To feel something other than alone and sad. But to say so would have been to betray Alan, so I just shook my head and left it to Kirk to interpret.

I already suspected that, unlike me, he had a lifetime of sexual experience, and I considered this as we lay together in the bleached, soft-worn sheets of the hotel bed. Kirk leaned on his elbow smiling down at me. It was a funny sort of smile. Thoughtful and affectionate. I could tell that he did genuinely like me, care about me, and my remaining doubt, uncertainty eased. I knew that nothing would happen that I didn't want to happen.

"I wasn't there," I said. "When Alan died. I was supposed to be there, but Mr. Gardener wasn't feeling good so he asked me if I could go to an estate sale for him. So I did. Alan was playing softball. The crew at WFLK versus the classical music station in Harrisonburg. One of those charity events, you know? It was a beautiful day. Bright and sunny. It was March, and you could feel that spring had arrived right on time."

Kirk was half lying against me, slowly stroking my collarbone with his thumb. If it had been anyone but Kirk, I would have felt self-conscious and ugly. I don't get what fashion models are about because there's nothing beautiful in jutting bones and stretched-too-tight skin. But then, if it had been anyone but Kirk, I wouldn't be here. Kirk already knew more about me than friends I'd known for years, and this wasn't about trying to impress or seduce. It wasn't about anything more than getting through the night.

"Go on," he said.

"It's ridiculous." I was smiling at the same time tears filled my eyes. What was with all this crying? I'd gone from never crying to a complete crybaby. My faucet was stuck. I said, "He was struck by lightning. Out of a clear blue sky. He died almost instantly."

"I'm sorry, Flynn."

I nodded, acknowledging the sincerity of that. "It was a freak accident. An act of God. Someone even said to me, 'It's an act of God, so you mustn't be angry.'"

"I'd be angry."

I wiped impatiently at my eyes. "I am angry. What kind of God would do that? Of course I'm angry. And what's wrong with being angry? What's wrong with being *sad*?"

"Nothing."

"I don't want to be numb and I don't want to forget. And too bad if that makes other people uncomfortable."

Kirk rested his hand against the side of my face, tilted my head up, and kissed me. It gave me a jolt. I hadn't wanted to be kissed, that was too much like making love, but it was happening before I had time to recognize his intent. The strangeness of it held me quiet. The softness of Kirk's beard, the softness of his lips, the softness of his eyelashes. His mouth tasted of whisky, which surprised me because he hadn't had whisky at dinner. Mostly he did not taste like Alan, and that difference was startling and confusing.

I had never been kissed on the mouth by anyone who wasn't Alan.

Kirk drew back. His breath was warm against my face as he said, "It's okay to be angry, Flynn. It's okay to be sad. You're allowed." His hand moved to the back of my skull, and he guided my head to his chest, settling me. He stroked my hair.

My mouth tingled, though it had been the sweetest of kisses, intended to comfort not arouse. The fine, wiry hair on his broad chest tickled my nose. I listened to the strong, steady pound of Kirk's heart beneath my ear.

Strange. So strange.

I felt like I should talk about Alan, tell Kirk how we had grown up together, known each other all our lives, known from the first that we would always be together. I felt like I needed to keep Alan here with us, but uppermost in my mind were all the ways that Kirk was different from Alan. I couldn't seem to stop inventorying all those differences, even though I didn't want to notice, let alone compare.

But there was no avoiding it. Kirk was so much larger. Not just taller and broader, but muscular. His biceps, his thighs, his pecs were all big and hard. His stomach was of the washboard variety. And he was hairy. There was the beard, of course, but there was also that unruly mop. I smiled faintly remembering that there had been bits of leaves in his hair when we'd stood in the graveyard. His chest was furry and his arms and legs too. Undoubtedly his crotch was a bush, though he was courteously still wearing his pajama bottoms. I say courteously, but it was maybe a little disappointing too.

That dismayed realization forced me to stop and think. Why was I dismayed? I'd had it in the back of my mind when I'd come looking for Kirk. *Help me forget for tonight.* That's what I was asking, and Kirk was willing. But he was also letting me set the pace. So why not be honest about it?

I lifted my head and kissed him. He kissed me back at once, and I was again reminded of the unfamiliarity of his taste and his scent. But it wasn't unpleasant. He sort of smelled like pencil shavings. I smiled at that idea and Kirk smiled too, and kissed me harder.

Something melted inside me. He tasted sweet beneath the whisky, like honey and smoke. And he didn't smell like pencil shavings, it was more like cedar wood and mint.

Heat pooled in my belly, my cock felt heavy. I tentatively bumped my hips against Kirk's and he bumped back. I moaned into his mouth and he threw his leg over mine, pulling us closer, snugging our groins up against each other — as much as was possible giving the stretch and thrust of two now fully erect cocks.

Kirk's big hands splayed against my ass cheeks, pressing me closer still as we began to awkwardly hump. I could feel the hot imprint of his hands through the soft cotton of my briefs. That same soft cotton, rubbing against the sensitive head of my cock was driving me crazy. I wanted bare skin. I wanted my naked cock rubbing against his, wanted the feel of crisp hair and silky skin and hot wet release. I wanted Kirk to yank his bottoms down — and my briefs too, while he was at it.

This hit and miss bunting and bouncing against each other was frustrating and exciting all at the same time. Again I moaned into Kirk's mouth, and he groaned back a noise that could have been reassuring or encouraging or equally exasperated.

His leg tightened, his hand flattened on my backside, forcing me into his rhythm, and we fell into a more satisfying meter, the rough, clumsy friction assuaging that frantic tension instead of teasing it into greater knots.

Blood beat dizzily in my ears, my heart labored, my lungs burned, mostly proof of how totally out of shape I was. Kirk's hips rocked faster, he thrust harder, nuzzling the underside of my jaw, beneath my temple, the corner of my eye. It was moist and messy and overwhelming. Gratefully, I pushed back, craving more, more contact.

The mattress springs squeaked. The bed frame creaked. The frame knocked against the wall. Once, twice. *Let me in!* Three times.

Kirk made a strangled sound. His hand slid up to the small of my back, smoothing in a restless, feverish caress before his arm locked around me and he went rigid. I felt orgasm sweep through him before I ever felt that blaze of liquid heat through soggy cotton.

Oh God. I made a desperate sound, but it was okay. Kirk wasn't leaving me to stand outside on my own. Still shivering with his own release, he shifted, reaching down, and his big hand pushed through the fly of my dampened briefs, closing around my cock. He was at the wrong angle and my briefs were too tight, but Kirk was practiced. What a beautiful thing experience was. He made it work, pumping me with a couple of long, beautiful strokes, and then switching to quick, hard short strokes. I threw my head back, just riding it out, gratefully accepting his attentions.

And oh yes. There it was. That sensation like a charge of raw electricity crackling at the base of my spine. So long since I'd felt this. In fact, I had intended never to feel it again. But it was too late now, and it was almost frightening how intensely good it was, how fierce the pleasure as that buzz of feeling washed through my cock, my balls, the pit of my stomach...and every nerve, muscle, cell in my body caught light.

For those few seconds, I did forget. I felt incandescent. Clear and bright and alive again. I was sailing in sunlight. My heart was at peace and the sting in my eyes was, for once, nothing to do with sorrow.

For those few seconds.

Sounds of distress wove their way through my dreams.

I opened my eyes to a strange and utter darkness, a confused awareness that I was not alone. But also the clear understanding that I was not with Alan.

Kirk. I was with Kirk. I knew it because my dreams had not been dreams so much as a dozing reliving of the day's adventures. Kirk was part of those adventures.

I rolled over to face him, to face his motionless shape beneath the blankets. I could tell he was breathing hard, I could almost feel his heart pounding across the short distance between us, but the sounds he made...

Tiny, smothered sounds, not even loud enough to wake anyone from a normal sleep. The hair rose on my head.

Kirk was screaming in his sleep.

Behind the unconscious mask of his face, his firmly pressed lips and closed eyes, he was screaming. Like someone buried alive. Like someone trapped in a burning house or beneath an avalanche of ice. Screaming and screaming and screaming for help that would never come.

"Kirk," I whispered. I reached out to touch him.

The next thing I knew I was flat on my back, Kirk's forearm was crushing my throat like a steel bar, and I felt the blood thumping in my ears.

"Kkhh..." I had to fight to get that much sound out. Bright lights burst behind my eyes, I hit blindly at his head, connected with his ear, his jaw. It made no difference. "Kkhhk!"

Just as suddenly, the weight lifted. I could breathe again. I dragged in frantic gulps of sweet, bed-warmed air. The lamp flashed on, blinding me for an instant.

"Jesus Christ!" Kirk's voice was horrified. "Flynn?"

He knelt over me, hair standing up, eyes black with horror. "Are you —?" His voice gave out as though he'd run out of air. Which made two of us.

"Kay!" I squawked, scrambling back, out of reach. I leaned against the headboard, putting a hand to my pulverized throat muscles. I forced out, "I'm okay."

His mouth hung open stupidly, his eyes were huge, transfixed. "I don't know what...I'm sorry, Flynn. I'm..."

"It's okay." I had my breath back and it was easier to speak, although my throat muscles still felt squashed.

"Did I — are you hurt?" His voice still came in winded gulps. But then who knew how long he had been fighting for his life before I woke him up.

I shook my head.

"I didn't realize. I didn't know it was you."

"It's okay. My fault. I shouldn't have startled you." I couldn't stand to see Kirk look like that. So frightened and sick. He regarded his hands like they were malignant. "Kirk!" I put my hands over his. "I'm fine. Really. You didn't hurt me." My mistreated vocal cords cracked on the last word, which made him wince.

I laughed, which wasn't any better.

"I didn't remember you were here."

"I know. It's okay."

"I haven't had one of those in a long time."

"This trip would give anyone nightmares."

He risked another guilty, pained glance at me. "Flynn..." He shook his head.

That time my laugh sounded more natural.

Kirk didn't laugh. "I could have killed you."

Yeah, I'd noticed that. "You didn't. Didn't even hurt me, really."

He scrubbed his face with the heels of his hands and said in that same exhausted voice, "I'm sorry. You probably better sleep alone."

"No. Come on. I'm fine. I'm not worried."

"Maybe you should be."

"No, I shouldn't." I glanced at the clock on the bedside table. "Anyway, we've only got a couple more hours before we have to get up. Let's get some sleep while we can."

"I think I'll go work out." He sounded dull. Defeated.

"Kirk." I scooted over and wrapped my arms around him. I said against his hair. "Lie down with me. We're both tired. We're okay here."

I could feel how divided he was, but then he seemed to give in, his shoulders slumping, his body leaning against mine. I hugged him and then we moved slowly, wearily crawling beneath the sheets and blankets, Kirk taking my former spot, me taking his. He turned out the bedside lamp. He slid his arm beneath my shoulders. I wrapped mine over his chest.

I'm pretty sure I dozed off before he did.

"Maybe you could write a book about Ines," I called through the adjoining open door the next morning as we dressed and packed. "If the stories and legends are right, and ghosts want the truth to be known, well, a book would take care of that."

Kirk's voice floated back, "Except I'm a playwright."

"You could write a play."

"It doesn't work like that. I'd need someone to produce it." He appeared in the doorway, looking surprisingly rested for someone who'd spent a fairly action-packed night. "I guess I could try my hand at writing some kind of article about her. Maybe for a historical magazine? If you think that's what she wants."

I tossed my toothbrush into my kitbag which was already in my carryall. "I'm just going by what the experts say."

When Kirk didn't answer, I glanced at him. He was very still, his brown gaze fixed on my arms. With the drapes wide open and daylight flooding in — and me wearing only my jeans — the deep, ugly scars on my arms stood out in stark relief.

Kirk's eyes raised to mine. He said thickly, "That wasn't a cry for help."

"No." Sudden, ferocious rage flared inside me because I didn't want him to see or know that much, because for a few hours I had been unconsciously happy, because last night I had felt something for him and I was afraid to even consider the possibility of what that might mean. I smiled at him. "No, it wasn't. And when this fucking year is over, when these next fucking ten months are over and done, I'm going to finish the job."

There. It was said. Now we both knew the rules of engagement.

Kirk said very quietly, "Is that the agreement? The agreement you have with your parents?"

"That's it. I won't try to harm myself for one year. One more year. And in return they won't try to lock me up like I'm an animal."

Kirk swallowed, his gaze never wavering from mine, as though I were indeed a dangerous animal he was keeping at bay by will alone.

I said nastily, "Don't worry. It won't be on your watch."

The fact that he didn't answer, didn't respond, just kept staring at me, wordless and appalled, made me angrier still. "I'm not crazy," I said. "I'm not deranged, delusional or depressed. It's very simple. I don't want to live without Alan. I *won't* live without him. There isn't anything for me on this goddamned planet without him."

Kirk stirred, said, "It's still — I mean, it's not that long —"

"Really? Because it seems endless night to me." I summoned another of those no doubt alarming smiles. "I'm not going to feel any different in one year or one hundred years. If Alan is gone then I want off the planet too. That's all. It would be nice if people could respect that, but that's okay. I can wait a year."

And yet even as I said it, insisted it, an odd...weariness seemed to flood me, douse the bright flames of my fury, wash away my certainty.

Was I? Was I really going to kill myself? Was there really nothing left? More, was I really going to do that to the people who loved me, were fighting to save me? People *I* loved. If there was one thing I'd learned in the last twenty-four hours, it was how short life was — how long death — and how there was never enough love to go around.

Kirk was still standing there, motionless. I glanced at the clock and said shortly, "We should go."

He turned back to his room without a word.

We let the radio fill the silence between us on the drive back to Baton Rouge.

We were flying past the sign for the Myrtles Plantation when Linkin Park's "Shadow of the Day" came on.

Sometimes goodbye's the only way.

We listened without speaking to the lyrics. They seemed uncomfortably applicable, so it was a relief when Kirk leaned forward and snapped off the radio.

I glanced at him. He stared back at me with bleak eyes. I started to speak, but he beat me to it.

"Just so you don't misunderstand what I was saying last night. It's one thing to give yourself permission to grieve. It's another to let loss define your life. If you let the loss become more important than everything that went before, you make everything that went before meaningless."

"You don't know what you're talking about."

"The hell I don't."

"You don't know me. You didn't know Alan. You have no right to sit in judgment."

"You think you're the only person in the world who lost someone he loved? Jesus, Flynn. You keep saying you're not a kid, but that's the attitude of an egotistical child. Death is part of life."

I gripped the wheel so hard, my knuckles turned white. "And that's the stupidest comment people can make. *Death is part of life!* No, it's not. Death is death. It's the *end* of life. It's the end of everything."

"Everybody dies, Flynn. It's a scheduled part of the program. It's how the world is meant to work. Everybody eventually loses someone they love. It's sad. It's the way it is. It's life. You don't get to kill yourself because it hurts so much."

"Why the hell not?" I threw back. "If I was terminally ill, I guarantee most people would understand wanting to stop the pain."

"You're *not* terminally ill!" he shouted. "It's not the same thing and you know it. For Christ's sake! We wouldn't last as a species if we all killed ourselves every time we lost someone we loved."

I sucked in a sharp breath, but made myself speak calmly. "Look, Kirk, I like you," I said. "I don't want to fight with you. You don't get to have an opinion on this."

"The hell I don't!"

I shook my head, determined not to continue the conversation. I had enough on my mind without arguing this out with Kirk. Why hadn't I kept my mouth shut? Now we had this between us, and I wanted his friendship. It was sort of unsettling to realize how much I'd come to rely on it.

He faced forward again, staring out the windshield, and I hoped that perhaps the conversation was over. But no. He said, "So if you had died, are you saying you'd have wanted Alan to kill himself?"

"Of course not!" I glared at him. "This isn't about what Alan would want or what Alan would do."

Alan would never have considered taking his own life. Had our positions been reversed, he'd have been devastated, but he'd have plowed through all the regular stages of grief and finally managed to accept. In time he'd have moved on. I'd have *wanted* that for him. I'd have wanted Alan to be happy again.

I wished it *had* been me and not Alan. Not least because Alan would have been so much better at living without me than I was at living without him.

"What do you think Alan would say if he could hear you now?"

"Shut the hell up, Kirk!" I yelled, forgetting about my intention to refuse to engage him on this. "Have the brains not to argue with me when I'm driving! That's what he'd say."

He didn't reply.

I waited. Risked a look his way. He was staring out the side window, but he must have felt my gaze because he turned his head and gave me a long, dark look.

"Grow the fuck up, Flynn," Kirk said.

Somehow the wintry disappointment in his eyes hurt a lot worse than the words.

CHAPTER SIXTEEN

On the flight home Kirk resorted to in-flight service and I stared numbly out the windows at the miles and miles of white clouds, the snowfields of heaven.

Back in Connecticut the snowfields were grayer and starting to melt around the edges.

We reached the house a little after eleven o'clock at night. Kirk parked in the shed on his half of the house, and we got our bags and trudged around to the front, letting ourselves inside.

The hall light was still burning, just as we'd left it. There was no sign of any intruder, human or otherwise. But it felt…wrong. I could feel that familiar pall. That chill sense of depression, anxiety, loss. It wasn't me. It was a relief to recognize that. For once I was a sufferer, not a carrier.

I looked at Kirk, really looked at him for the first time since we'd left Louisiana. He looked back at me. There were lines of fatigue in his face. He looked like he'd aged years during the past hours.

I put down my carryall on the bottom step of the staircase. "Well. I guess I should, er, get out there and have a word with Ines," I said, and as usual, when worried, I sounded too flippant, too off-hand. The fact was, I was scared to death.

Kirk stood in the center of the hall watching me. "Leave it, Flynn. At least leave it for tomorrow. Don't try anything tonight."

"I wish I could." I wished, too, that I had spent less time on our flight brooding over everything Kirk had said to me, and more time thinking about what I was going to do once we got home and I had to face the mirror. And Ines.

"Of course you can," Kirk said impatiently. "You said it yourself, this may all be resolved tomorrow anyway."

"What if it isn't? What if I miss the window on this? What if it has to be tonight?" Kirk was looking at me like I wasn't making sense, and anxiety goaded me into snapping, "I don't think Ines is cycling through her manic phase, Kirk. I don't think this is a mood swing or hormones or the pull of the moon. I think she's here to stay unless we figure this out. And I don't think leaving the mirror bundled up in a shed is going to stop her from appearing tonight. Tonight of all nights?"

"Then go to a hotel."

I couldn't believe he'd said it. "*You* go to a hotel, Kirk."

Anger lit his eyes. "You don't know what the hell you're doing. You don't know what you're tampering with, Flynn. You don't have a goddamned plan."

"Sure I do. I'll tell her you're going to write a news article and set the record straight." I was half joking. Half not.

Kirk didn't see any part of the joke. "Goddamn it, Flynn," he yelled. His voice sounded hoarse as though he'd been shouting at me for hours. And maybe in his thoughts, he had. "You keep saying you're not crazy, but *this* is crazy."

I yelled back, "The situation is crazy. What do you want from me? I didn't ask for this. I *don't* know what I'm doing. But I don't believe it's a coincidence that we're back here tonight on the anniversary of Ines's death. This *is* the night, Kirk. I can feel it."

He was right though. I didn't know what I was doing. I didn't have a plan. And I *was* every bit as afraid as him. More. What if Ines took me over again? What if Ines did something to me that got me locked up in Silver Springs permanently? Could she kill me? Could ghosts kill?

What if Ines did something that kept me from ever seeing Alan again?

"Listen to me." Kirk reached out as though to put his hand on my shoulder, but he stopped himself. "I've been thinking about this. We'll send the mirror back."

"Send it back where?"

"To Bellehaven. Donate it to the museum."

"You're going to leave Daphne and Maryann to deal with Ines? Seriously?"

"They won't have to deal with anything. The museum is closed at night. Besides, you said it yourself, neither of them would notice a ghost unless it was standing in front of them waving its arms."

I considered this. Bellehaven was Ines's home. Maybe that *was* what she wanted? She was buried there. Her baby was buried there. Maybe the trouble had started by taking the mirror away from Bellehaven? Maybe Kirk was also right about the supernatural not manifesting itself to people who weren't open to it? Maybe

Daphne and Maryann would be happily oblivious of Ines's presence. It was true that Ines's manifestations would take place after hours.

Or maybe, once she was home, Ines would never appear again.

I chewed my lip, thinking. Yes. Maybe this was the solution. Send Ines home.

A temporary solution anyway.

And what was time to someone who had been waiting a century?

Waiting a century for what?

"What are you thinking?" Kirk asked, frowning.

What did a ghost want?

Once upon a time Ines hadn't been a ghost. She had been a woman, the victim of a great injustice. So what did a woman like that want?

Justice? Vengeance? Reparation?

What did someone who had suffered a wrong that could never be put right, want?

Ines must want something or she wouldn't still be lingering between worlds.

"Flynn?"

I looked up out of the jumble of my thoughts. "Let's ask Ines what she wants," I said. "Let's just get it over with. Do you have a flashlight?"

"Have you heard *anything* I've said to you?"

I considered him for a moment. His hair was standing on end again. I took in his dark, hollowed gaze, the compressed line of his mouth. I remembered suddenly how soft and tender his mouth had been on mine only the night before. I said, "I think I've heard every single thing you've said to me, Kirk."

His eyes flickered and just for an instant there was something unguarded in his hard, fierce face. After a tense pause he muttered, "I must be crazier than you."

"Flattery will get you nowhere." I sat down on the step next to my bag and waited while Kirk disappeared into his rooms. He returned a short while later with one of those big, heavy duty flashlights.

I raised my brows. "Wow. Do you mine for coal in your spare time?"

He merely looked pained, leading the way outside. My heart was galloping as we stepped onto the porch. Our footsteps on the wooden slats sounded as loud as a crack. The cold, clear night air felt refreshing after the stale, unhealthy atmosphere of the house. It helped calm me down a little. I drew a couple of deep breaths.

Kirk probably thought I was hyperventilating, but he didn't say anything.

"Thanks for coming with me," I said to him as we went down the steps.

He gave a curt shake of his head, which could have been any variation on the theme of *don't mention it*. I was glad Kirk was with me, though. Glad he hadn't tried harder to discourage me or make this any more difficult than it already was.

We tramped through what was left of the snow around the house to the shed on the east wing of the house.

"Have you thought about what you'll do if she comes out of the mirror again?"

I shook my head. "Run like hell?"

I heard everything he didn't say, and I replied, "All I know is, I'm not going to bed to wake up with Ines standing over me. I'd rather confront her while I'm awake."

"Yeah, well, good morning Vietnam," Kirk muttered. He unfastened the padlock and opened the tall, wooden door. The hinges screeched so loudly they probably startled Ines.

The beam of the flashlight played over broken furniture, a row of tarnished and badly dented milk canisters, a wheelbarrow with a flat tire...and came at last to rest on the tarped-and-roped outline of the mirror.

I swallowed and hoped the noise wasn't audible.

Kirk set the flashlight on a battered trunk. He moved past me and began to undo the ropes bundling the tarp. I went to join him. My hands felt cold and stiff.

Finally the ropes fell away, and Kirk dragged the tarp off the mirror. The glass surface winked and shone in the glare of the flashlight like a big jewel. Whether it was its angle or the poor lighting, none of the items in the shed were reflected in its bright, blank eye.

I looked at Kirk. His features looked chiseled from stone, his eyes shining like jet in the eerie light.

"It's okay," I whispered. Why the hell was I whispering? I said more strongly, "I'm okay now. You don't have to stay."

He actually laughed. "If you think I'm leaving you, think again."

That was a huge relief, though I didn't think there was a lot Kirk could do against a ghost. Unless he was carrying one of his trusty salt shakers. I had to swallow a nervous and inappropriate titter. I took a deep breath and knelt in front of the mirror, feeling a little silly and a lot self-conscious. There was no flooring and the ground was damp and hard beneath the dirty and sketchy covering of hay.

"Turn out the light," I said after a moment.

The flashlight clicked off leaving us in instant and complete darkness.

I stared at the mirror. The minutes passed. Kirk stood soldier still, a shadowy outline behind me.

I could hear his watch ticking.

Seconds.

Minutes.

Maybe we should have tried to hire a psychic? Or at least brought a Ouija board with us.

I could feel Kirk behind me though he was so quiet I couldn't even hear him breathing.

I began to hope I was wrong. Maybe Ines wouldn't show. Maybe she had other plans. Maybe time was irrelevant to a ghost and tonight wasn't any more important to Ines than any other night. I wanted nothing more than to get up, lock the shed, and go into the house with Kirk.

Maybe he could share some of that whisky. Maybe after a drink or two I could explain to him. Explain that even *I* wasn't so stupid and selfish that I didn't understand that it was different now. In November I hadn't understood what I was doing. Nobody could blame me for that because, let's face it, I had been totally and clinically *wack*. But it was different now. I was different. And I did understand that. And I didn't want to hurt anybody. It was just…

Behind us, the shed door creaked in the still night air. The moonlight flickered on the blind eye of the mirror.

No, the flicker was within the mirror. I heard Kirk's quiet intake of breath. My heart jumped. My palms were instantly sweaty.

Game time.

I closed my eyes and concentrated as I had the first night when I had believed, hoped, that spark of light was Alan.

I let my mind go blank, let go of my fear, opened myself to…

She was there. Right there. It was hard not to recoil from that black miasma. My heart felt tight in my chest, my lungs too small for the amount of air I needed.

I opened my eyes.

Ines filled the mirror just as I had seen her the first time, beautiful, mocking, malevolent.

"Ines?" My voice sounded too loud. I leaned forward, staring in at her, staring until she saw me too. She did see me. Her eyes widened. We gazed at each other. I licked my lips. My voice cracked as I said, "You have to go to the light."

She seemed to fade a little, dissolve into the swirling mist around her. Or was she the mist? I couldn't tell. At moments her features were as clear as if she stood in front of me, and then they seemed to melt away, her eyes and mouth becoming no more real than smoke in water.

"You're dead, Ines," I said. "You have to go into the light."

The shed door swung shut with a bang that shook the entire structure. We were closed into pitch blackness.

"Don't tell her she's dead," Kirk said in a low voice.

"She is dead, though."

The entire shed began to shake. The tin roof rattled. The boards groaned. The milk canisters clanked against each other.

"Flynn!"

"Ines," I rushed on, raising my voice to be heard above the crack and pop of separating wood and metal. "We know the truth. The truth is..." *Out there?* "Known. To us. To others. What happened to you isn't a secret. It can't be hidden anymore."

What *had* happened to her? Did we even know?

The shed shook harder. Something fell from the ceiling and hit the ground with a crash. A lantern? The row of milk canisters rattled like knuckle bones.

I said desperately, "We're going to tell the truth. Others will know too. Everything is okay now."

Or not.

I closed my eyes. Forced myself to focus. I tried to project soothing, kind thoughts. *It's over. It's all over. We're going to tell your story. We're going to put it in the papers. We're going to write a book. We're going to put on a play.* My frantic thoughts rushed on but mostly I was fighting the urge to jump up and run.

This was a mistake. What had I imagined I could accomplish? Trying to face this wall of rage was like standing in front of a tidal wave. Kirk had been right. There was no fixing this. Our only possible chance was to get rid of the mirror. Send it away. Lock it up good and tight.

I raised my voice. "Do you want to go home? Do you want to go back to Bellehaven?"

As suddenly as it had started, the commotion stopped.

A board fell out of the wall. Through the gap I could see the swaying branches of the dead bushes. The scratch of twigs against the wall slowly registered.

I looked back at Kirk. I couldn't see his expression, but I could tell all his attention was on the mirror. Reluctantly, I turned back to face the mirror. Ines was there, large as life, filling the frame. She was so close I could see the tiny beauty mark next to her mouth, the sooty length of her eyelashes, the tiny silver cross around her long, white neck. I had the horrible feeling she was about to step through. I wasn't sure I could handle that.

My mouth was so dry, the words felt sticky. "Is that what you want? To go home? To be with your baby?"

The mirror went black. It was as though Ines had turned out the light.

"Is that it?" I whispered. "Do we just send the mirror back?"

I felt Kirk start to answer, but then the shed began to shake again. Violently. The tin roof lifted as though it was about to tear away, and in the rift, I glimpsed starlight.

The glass in the mirror seemed to turn an eerie silvery green.

"That can't be good," Kirk said.

As we watched, the mirror started to rock. It banged against the wall of the shed, like a heavy hand knocking on a flimsy door.

Bang. Bang. Bang.

Each time the mirror tipped forward, it threw flashes of light against the heaving ceiling and floor like green lightning strikes. It had a kind of hypnotic beauty to it. Pockets of sky and stars were illumined in those brief flares as the roof rippled and tugged.

From a distance I heard Kirk yell something. The next thing I knew, he had hold of me and was dragging me out of the shed. We landed in a mound of dirty snow. Kirk's hand was still fastened in my collar. His other hand gripped my arm with bruising force.

The shed door slammed shut behind us.

I jackknifed up, wiped snow off my face, and spluttered, "What the *hell*, Kirk?"

"Did you not see that goddamned mirror nearly fall on you?"

No.

No, I hadn't seen that. I'd been busy thinking about the roof falling on me.

I looked back at the shed which was gradually settling down again. "Oh God. Now I have to make myself go back in there."

"You are not going in there," Kirk said with finality. "I gave your father my word nothing would happen to you. I'm going to keep that promise."

"That's not something you can promise. That's not something even *I* can promise. I have to go back in there. We can't leave it like this."

"If that mirror had landed on you, you'd have been killed."

"Then don't let the mirror fall on me." I stood, brushed the snow and dirt from my clothes. I stared down at him. "Look, I don't know why this is my problem, but it is my problem. Maybe it doesn't make sense, but I'm more certain every minute that it's up to me and no one else to fix this."

"Fix it how?" He practically howled the words, leaping to his feet and glaring at me. "In case you didn't notice, it wasn't going well in there."

"Because I don't know what I'm doing!"

"I noticed!"

"That doesn't mean I can give up."

I could see Kirk struggling with that, because he agreed with me, at least in principle. And we both knew it.

I looked back at the shed. "I think maybe I *am* doing something right because she isn't out of the mirror."

"She doesn't need to be out of the mirror. You came to her."

"Or maybe that's it."

"For all we know, she only speaks French. She may not even understand what you're saying to her. You may simply be antagonizing her. Did you ever think of that?"

"She understands. It isn't just about the words. She can feel what I'm telling her."

I listened to the echo of my words and an idea, a very small idea, sparked to life. "Okay. I'm going back in. You don't have to come —"

"Save your breath," Kirk growled.

When I opened the door to the shed, I thought maybe Ines had gone. Such an ordinary blend of scents greeted my nose: diesel and moldering hay and long ago animals. It was absolutely silent. The mirror reflected our tense shapes in the doorway.

"Maybe she blew a fuse," Kirk said.

"No," I said slowly. "She's here."

I could feel that she was there, although I couldn't have explained how. I just… knew. Just as I knew that it was my responsibility to deal with her.

I crossed the length of the shed and knelt before the mirror once more. Over my shoulder I said, "Can you shut the door again?"

Kirk pulled the door shut.

The dark felt too close and strange. Like there were things I couldn't see crowding beside me. I closed my eyes and tried to think only of Ines. But this time I tried to think of Ines herself and not how we could get rid of her.

No, I didn't know her full story. I didn't know if she'd had an affair or if she'd driven her husband to suicide or if she'd committed suicide. It didn't matter. What I did know for sure was…

Pain. Loss.

My breath caught. I kept my eyes closed tight and just let myself feel. That was it. I didn't need to know the details in order to be sorry for everything she'd suffered. All that anger, all that pain, all that loss. I understood that. What I didn't understand was how did anyone survive that? How did anyone let go? Move on?

How?

But…I did know.

"Flynn." Kirk's voice was low, urgent.

I opened my eyes. Ines floated in the mirror again. Her hand was outstretched, fingertips brushing her side of the glass, as she tried to reach through.

I raised my hand and pressed it to the glass, covering Ines's. The glass felt cold. Shockingly cold. Somewhere behind me I heard Kirk's protest, felt him moving to stop me, but I didn't let myself think about Kirk. I didn't think about anyone except Ines. I stopped resisting, stopped fighting, simply opened to her, thinking only *sorry. So sorry.*

I shoved against the glass and my hand seemed to slip through, like pushing through gel. No, like water. Like cold, thick, deep water. I saw my hand touch Ines's smaller one.

I felt a kind of cool charge, a wash of energy and light, a current flowing between us...

And then a bewildering rush of images, a stream of memories that were not my own. Too much, too fast, like a flip book of daguerreotypes. The pictures barely made sense. I was seeing Ines but I was also seeing through Ines. So I saw Ines preening at her reflection as she tried on a new hat. And I saw Edward's face as he forced himself on her. I saw the pale island of her belly as she struggled to give birth. I saw the small, wrinkled face of her baby. But it wasn't just likenesses. I was feeling everything Ines felt. I felt tenderness and grief and rage and laughter and hunger. I touched velvet and smelled tobacco and tasted sherry. I heard music and a roar of voices and talking.

I tried to stay calm, focused, but it was hard to fight the panic that came with the idea that I was losing myself in this torrent of someone else's consciousness. I was being swept away. I tried to hold fast to empathy and openness, but instinctively I began to struggle, to try and break free, get my head above water.

Water.

And then something seemed to snap. Everything was moving slowly, we were back in real time, and I could feel Ines running, her heart hammering, her lungs on fire, feet sliding and slipping on rocks and grass as she fled. I could feel her terror like a weight on my chest, smothering me.

They were right behind her.

The sun looked red in the late afternoon sky, it cast an ominous glow over house and hill. The grass beneath her feet looked bleached and gray. She wore satin slippers and she felt every stone, every twig. Her night dress caught on one of the azalea bushes. She ripped free and stumbled on. Tears blinded her.

"Flynn!" someone yelled from very far away.

If she could get down to the woods, she could hide, and then later she could make her way to the Fitzgerald place. Sarah would help her get home. Home to New Orleans.

Her foot slipped on the slimy rock and she went down. I felt the shock of the cold water, the rush of green and silver bubbles. The wet nightdress tangled around her legs. She couldn't swim. Dank, fishy water filled her nose and mouth. She clawed the surface, grabbing at slimy lily pads.

Beyond the edge of the pool her pursuers had gathered. They ringed the bank, watching her.

I saw it all. I felt it all. Time slowed to a crawl. Her desperation and terror were mine. But I was not her. I was the other one. Flynn. I held to that knowledge and waited while she fought. With a pang, I recognized the moment Ines stopped struggling. Her vision went dark. The connection between us broke. At last I was able to tear free. I struck out for the surface.

I came back to the present coughing and choking. I was flat on my back in a weird smelling shed. Kirk gripped my shoulders, and he was saying, "Flynn? Flynn?" Over and over.

"She didn't kill herself. They let her drown."

"Flynn? Can you hear me?"

I caught my breath. "I'm okay."

I wasn't drowning. I wasn't even wet.

"What the hell happened?" Kirk sounded shaken. He still hung onto me with that reassuring fierceness. "I thought you had a seizure."

I shook my head. I rolled away from him, pushed up to my hands and knees, and stumbled to my feet. Kirk rose too, steadying me as I swayed.

"Do you feel that?" I asked him.

"Feel what?"

I freed myself, staggering over to the mirror. Kirk's flashlight beam eerily highlighted my white face and shadowy form. I didn't remember him turning the light back on, but it now revealed Kirk's wide eyes, the broken pieces of furniture scattered around us, a beautiful and very old, but very ordinary mirror.

"You don't feel that?" I said. I turned back to Kirk. "She's gone. Ines is gone. Really gone this time. It's over."

"I saw it," Kirk said.

"What did you see?"

He shook his head, and I didn't think he was going to answer. Then he said, "You touched her. You reached through the mirror and touched her. The light went out in the mirror and you had what looked to me like a convulsion." His hand still held mine. His skin was like ice, his fingers not quite steady. "I thought you were dying."

"No." I looked at the mirror again. "I saw Ines die. I felt it." I shivered. "I heard you calling to me." Had hearing Kirk call my name helped me find my way back? I wasn't sure. I couldn't begin to fully understand what had happened.

I put my hand to the mirror's glass. It felt cold, but it was the normal, expected chill. Nothing strange. Nothing supernatural.

"How long did it last?" I asked.

"A few seconds. No more than a minute."

It had felt like hours to me.

"I don't know what they were going to do to her. Maybe they were just going to question her. Or maybe they were going to arrest her. But they let her drown, Kirk. They stood there and watched her drown."

"Just take it easy, slow down."

"I saw everything. I saw her whole life here. There, I mean. I saw her life at Bellehaven. I watched it go by like a film at high speed. Only I could feel everything. I could experience everything."

More than I had wanted. A lot more than I had wanted.

"Then you know what happened to her?"

"I-I feel like I do. It's kind of confused. I don't think she had an affair. I don't think she stopped loving Edward until the end, but at the end she did hate him. She couldn't forgive him for his betrayal. Except." I rubbed my forehead. I didn't want to remember this, but it was there with all the rest of it. "When she was dying she was calling for him. All I know is she was in so much pain. But the pain turned to fury. Maybe that was it. Her rage at the unfairness of everything that happened to her."

Kirk's wary and wondering expression watched me in the mirror. "How did you do it?" he asked at last. "How did you get her to let go?"

I glanced up, turned to face him. "It wasn't what I thought. It was the opposite of what I thought."

"What was? What happened?

"I'm probably not explaining this well."

"How did you know to do what you did? How did you know to reach out to her?"

I said hesitantly, "I guessed that it wouldn't be any different for the spirit of someone dead than the spirit of someone alive. I guessed…"

"What?"

I shook my head, trying to clear it. I felt…not confused, but there was so much to sort through, to try and make sense of. I said, "I finally realized you don't help someone, you don't heal someone's pain by closing your eyes, by turning away, by running from them."

He opened his mouth, said at last in an odd voice, "How did you work that out?"

I recognized how much I liked his face, how much I had come to like him. I felt my mouth curving into a smile. Because I liked him so much — and because he didn't begin to know how much he had done for me.

I told him the simple truth. "I didn't. You did."

* * * * *

I was brushing my teeth, still avoiding looking directly at my reflection in the bathroom mirror, when I heard the knock on my door.

I spat, rinsed, spat again and went to open the door.

Kirk was in the process of turning away, but he turned back when the door swung open. He looked self-conscious.

"Were you in bed?"

I shook my head. "On my way."

"I meant to give you this a while ago." He handed me a very old photograph, curled and yellowed at the edges.

I stared at the portrait of a slight young man in Victorian clothing. He had pale hair, light eyes, and a beard. Except for the beard and the old fashioned clothing, it could have been a picture of me.

Puzzled, I turned the photo over. There was nothing on the back. No indication of who the man in the photo might be. I looked inquiringly at Kirk.

"Your uncle gave me a book about a year ago. That photograph was stuck between the pages. I only discovered it a couple of months ago, after he died."

"It could be me."

"Yeah. It's the image of Winston too, a much younger version of him, of course. But the photo is too old to be Winston. Maybe it's your great-great-grandfather or a great-great-great-uncle?" He shrugged. "I thought you'd probably want it back."

"Thank you." I studied the photo again.

"Is something wrong?"

"Hm?" I raised my gaze to Kirk's frowning one. "No. It's just weird. So weird."

"The resemblance, you mean? It's a little uncanny, but some families do manage to stamp that genetic watermark on every generation."

"Yeah but…"

"But?"

"I'm adopted."

"You're…" For once Kirk looked genuinely floored.

"Adopted. Yeah, I was adopted when I was a baby." I couldn't help laughing at his expression.

"That *is* a little weird," he said very mildly at last.

I laughed again. "But not, you have to admit, the weirdest thing that's happened tonight."

"Maybe not. No. True." He smiled, looked at the photo, looked at me.

I smiled too. "Anyway, thank you. I do want this."

Kirk nodded.

We neither of us moved.

It shouldn't have been hard. It was. I said, "Well, thank you again for everything you did. Not just tonight, but since I moved in here."

Kirk said, "No thanks necessary."

"Goodnight."

"Night, Flynn."

I closed the door softly.

I studied the browned photograph. "That's a very nice waistcoat, Great-Grandpappy," I remarked. I checked the back of the photo again, but of course no information or date had magically appeared during the past minute. "Who are you?" I asked softly.

The face so like my own smiled wryly back for the camera.

For that matter, who was *I*?

When I finally climbed into bed I could hear Kirk playing his guitar downstairs.

I turned out the lamp and stared up at the pattern of moonlight on the ceiling. The bed was warm and more comfortable than I remembered. I thought I would sleep well that night.

After a time I closed my eyes and listened to Kirk strumming. Not random chords, not a haphazard scattering of notes, just a slow, tentative introduction to an unfamiliar melody.

ACKNOWLEDGEMENT

It takes a village. Or a publishing house. Or an awful lot of good friends and colleagues. Thank you to LB Gregg, Laura, S.C. Wynne, K.B. Smith, Will, Caroline, Keren, and last but not least, Janet.

And thank you for buying this book.

ABOUT THE AUTHOR

A distinct voice in gay fiction, multi-award-winning author JOSH LANYON has been writing gay mystery, adventure and romance for over a decade. In addition to numerous short stories, novellas, and novels, Josh is the author of the critically acclaimed Adrien English series, including The Hell You Say, *winner of the 2006 USABookNews awards for GLBT Fiction. Josh is an Eppie Award winner and a three-time Lambda Literary Award finalist.*

Follow Josh on Twitter, Facebook, and Goodreads
Find other Josh Lanyon titles at www.joshlanyon.com.